Praise for The

"In *The Shrieking of Nothing*, set in the year 2220, the detective Edwina Casaubon narrates her journey to find Momo, a missing young man who leads her and her partner through a world that is gorgeously fantastical and futuristic, yet grounded in real human emotions, familiar belief systems, and the forever mysteries of this universe we inhabit. A straightforward detective novel wrapped up in a spiritual quest, *The Shrieking of Nothing* is a gripping, moving account of the hopes and limitations of our desire for transformation and salvation, both of our spiritual and physical worlds. Simply beautiful."

— Paula Bomer, author of *Tante Eva*

"If not quite a key to all mythologies, Jordan A. Rothacker's *The Shrieking of Nothing* seems nevertheless a key to many, and offers us something wonderful, vivid and strange: a portrait of life after capitalism in the form of a sinuous noir that plumbs our deepest, most visionary impulses. Echoes abound—of J.G. Ballard and Philip K. Dick, Walter Tevis and Steve Erickson—but the vision here is wholly Rothacker's own, and the result is transfixing."

— Matthew Specktor, author of *Always Crashing the Same Car*

"In Jordan A. Rothacker's intriguing and insightful murder mystery, he reminds us that even in a utopian society where an enlightened population chooses the gods they wish to emulate, there are lost souls driven to commit acts of violence and the need for heroes to pursue them."

— Mickey Dubrow, author of *American Judas* and *Bulletproof*

"Author, Jordan A. Rothacker, deftly tows that fine line between levity and lament, exploring what David Bowie called 'the great salvation of bullshit faith' with a clear note of warning, a strong dose of empathy, and dare I say, hope. This novel is a strange fascination, indeed!"

— Lillah Lawson, author of *Monarchs Under the Sassafras Tree, So Long, Bobby,* and *Doomed Girls of Jefferson*

"Rothacker takes us back to the enthralling post-Kapital-death world of domed Atlanta and leaves no path toward enlightenment unturned in this harrowing whodunit. Sacred Detectives Edwina Casaubon, and Rabbi Jakob 'Thinkowitz' Rabbinowitz are once again called to action when a strange disappearance leads to even stranger murders. Though the planet outside of the dome is dead— murdered by greed—the vibrant society within has evolved such that belief, faith, and emulation are as free and varied as Atlanta's citizens. To tread the Sacred and Profane byways and intersections with Casaubon and Rabbinowitz is to explore humanity's traditions and intentions with Rothacker as your keen, caring, and enthusiastic guide."

— William M. Brandon III, author of *Eternity*

"Jordan A. Rothacker's *The Shrieking of Nothing* is a crisp, Promethean jaunt, sure to be enjoyed by fans of both Tech-noir and the original stuff."

— Andy Rusk, professional stuntman, stunt coordinator on the FX show *Atlanta*

"Fun, fast, and smart, *The Shrieking of Nothing* is a gift and a question. Though Rothacker's prose is taut and his worldbuilding singular, it's the book's clever central mystery that makes it unputdownable."

— Mike McClelland, author of *Gay Zoo Day*

"Whatever Jordan Rothacker writes, wherever the setting, whatever cast of characters, however how high the moon, or low the tide, whether in the future or in the past, whether in Paris, Atlanta, or Nowheresville, whether the world is sacred or profane... you will find the same crackling prose, the same head-spinning wit, the bacchanalian glee, the rapier-like dialogic play, and the same heartfelt yearning for the truth, and for human connection. You open his books; you'll open your head. The Shrieking is more like singing, and the Nothing, is definitely something."

— Reginald McKnight, author of *He Sleeps*, and *White Boys*

"Rothacker's words, like graveled crystal, tumbled in a kaleidoscopic lens: words are flowers, rocks, odors morphing into ever-changing stain-glass patterns of image and ideas. Jordan is a Cosmonik stringing together shards of cold technology with immediate shades of the sensual. Divine beings born of tropical mythologies are introduced, holding hands with prophets of the profane, and invite the reader into this future world. Come inside and enjoy."

— Darius James, author of *Negrophobia*

Also by Jordan A. Rothacker

The Pit, and No Other Stories
And Wind Will Wash Away
My Shadow Book by Maawaam
The Death of the Cyborg Oracle
Gristle: weird tales

The Shrieking of Nothing

A Domed Atlanta Future Noir

Jordan A. Rothacker

SPACEBOY BOOKS

Denver, Colorado

Published in the United States by:
Spaceboy Books LLC
1627 Vine Street
Denver, CO 80206
www.readspaceboy.com

Cover features art by Sam Grant

ISBN: 978-1-951393-39-7
First printed October 2024

Author's Note

The Reader will have been best served to read the volume, *The Death of the Cyborg Oracle*, first. However, that is not essential for enjoying and understanding this narrative.

A New Day

There should be a pylon up there.

It's what I think whenever I'm here.

There really should be a pylon up there.

And this time I was running up there, up to up there. To the free space at the top of the rock, New Gibraltar, in the eastern domain of the Dome.

From the ground to the summit, it is about a mile on a steadily rising incline, this western slope. Treeless after the first rise, this dome-shaped mountain of stone is not quite dome-smooth, but it's northern face was smoothed by an early *us*, a pre-*us*, in the 21st century. A blank slate for projecting and reflecting colors and entertainment. A tabula rasa for everyone. This rock, this New Gibraltar, this mountain of stone.

I leapt an oblong chunk of granite, feeling a giddy glee for that moment aloft. Low, but aloft. Cooler air breathing through my carbon fiber boots, and then the soft-squish-rubber landing. A little breeze into the collar of my navy blue, zipped-up jump suit. And I kept on running.

When I run like this, I have to distract my mind. On this day and place, it wasn't difficult. The lack of a pylon anywhere at the summit loomed over my head and upon my mind. The lack loomed. The bald head of the rock shined.

And it is just a rock, a pluton, an intrusion of igneous rock out of the soil's top layer. In actuality, a multitude of rocks in amalgam. Like leaves of grass. Granite in combination with quartz monzonite, granodiorite, and pink granite. The rock and rocks, mostly blanched and seer.

Welled-up, 350 million years past, magma from our core to cool here. When this dome was young, Africa touched our shores. One world of many.

Up, I jumped, climbed, and ran over a series of inclines with regular sub-summits. I avoided stretches of ramps and steps, reenforcing my training, feeling and honing my body. I relished the hopeful flora, reaching and poking through cracks and crags, life prevailing through this nesting dome within a greater dome. I steadied my breath through naming.

Wildflowers. So many subsets. Agrimonia gryposepala. Yellow daisies. Dewberry. Thimbleberry. Small bugbane. Least bluets. Then little rock pools and plants. Gratiola amphiantha... pool sprite... snorklewort...

From an awkward hop, the tip of my boot landed on the corner of a low rock that looked like a truncated cone cupping a shallow, dark pool. The petals of a snorklewort in bloom along the water's surface were ground by my boot into the rock, and the scent—subtle, pungent, bitter—rose up to my passing olfactory awareness.

On the wind, I caught relief through some rosewood, a waft of someone's body oil, then back into the thick of life. I jumped into, and ran up through, a crowd. I ducked and climbed around casual hikers, vista-viewers, and some other people expressing their bodies in a similar manner as my own, but at different speeds.

The scents enveloped me, and I embraced them. Sour, tangy, onions and cabbage through glandular filters, and musks and pheromones and Somber Hope and the sweat of panicky guilt, that urge to implode and the subsequent shivers, and still then there was the smell of breath, sticky saliva of lips parting, mucus drying as corners were pulled into a smile and for a tenth of a second it was right by my ear, a face in the crowd, and I felt-it-heard-it-smelt-it, and then nothing but my boots beating against the rock, the rocks, up steep, off the steps, out of the crowd, up rock. And I craned my neck towards the not-too-distant summit.

There should be a pylon up there.

I said to myself between breaths.

See, Dear Reader of the Future, we are not without our faults. Hopefully, you have solved such social difficulties. And the greatest utilitarian good for all trumps individualist wants and practices, no matter how holy. No matter how Sacred. The Greater Good is the Greater Good. But I apologize for the tautology.

It was deemed Sacred Space. But not without a struggle. Not without debate. So many called it sacred. So many divine points of contact and correspondence. The loudest voices, most impassioned and devout, justified the social need in this Sacred way.

And now a Sacred Place is a place of structural weakness. A concession for the Sacred, a compromise for the Profane.

We are all trained in Dome-Care; every citizen able to aid in the maintenance of the Dome. Everyone trained for the Greater Good.

We live on hope. It's a Somber Hope, but hope is a practice, and it is a sustenance. Every day we hope, and as we live and prevail, we are reminded of why.

And today there was a call to City Safety, Sacred Division. I took the call and replayed the recording of it, studying, before heading here. It's been a long time since there was a call to Sacred. I felt the urgency in the call, the worry. For all my enjoyment in feeling my body in action like this someone's life depended on me.

There was one more landing before the summit. And then up. My swift-booted-feet beat hard, and my brow welcomed a breeze.

There standing at the top, the summit edge, was a dark pillar, a sharp, dark angle cut across its own top. The dark pillar pulsed within a circling nimbus of light from the white sun high behind and filtered through the Dome.

The last rise. The sharpest incline. I trod hard and up against the rock and rise. Running up. Right at the dark figure.

We Met Upon a Hill

"Casaubon, where you gonna run to? All on that day. We got to run to the rock!"

I've been studying and training. Body and mind. I could never *be* him, but I understood the need to be a fuller participant. A partner. To rise and meet him, and his abilities, to attempt that rise. Like *we* rose to meet the impossible. Like *we* rose the Dome. RESURGA, our rallying cry.

He was cheery and serene. His smile jovial and sly. His coat of charcoal grey, organic fiber, no touch-up tech. His black fedora cut sharp and jaunty. He was my partner, Sacred Detective Jakob "Thinkowitz" Rabbinowitz.

I bent and panted. Sweat dripped from my brow before I sopped it with my left sleeve. I knew he wasn't testing me, but I still wanted to pass.

"Is that... from... Bakkhai..."

I panted and sopped again between breathes and sweats and syllables.

"From...

"Euripi...

"des... ?"

And I was done. Riding away for a moment on endorphins and dopamine, my favorite highs secondary only to the rapt awe I felt in exploring the City, and vibing the palpable belief and electric devotion of believers that pierced me in sympathetic, empathic, and psycho-sexual ways.

This view brought that awe too. It was a high clearing in a cluttered skyline. On top of this pallid rock, in an empty space without a pylon there was an energy and an indescribable sensation of freedom. I looked out at what we have wrought. At the towers. At all the colors touched-up across every public surface. I looked out at the circling, green, snaky space of I-285. I wanted to cry and vomit.

"In all of your study, Casaubon. You mustn't neglect your Profane Prophets," Thinkowitz was emphatic, his smile sweet. "That was from Nina Simone. But I believe you must have been thinking about the line: *Sing glorying your god/in the thunder of drums!/To the mountains!/To the mountains!* Maybe even the translation by another Profane Prophet, the 21st century's Anne Carson."

I confirmed the correctness of his assumption; an action I dutifully—and often—performed as part of my partnership.

We took a moment unspoken to stand and feel and look around in silence.

"How was your run?" he asked.

My face answered for me with a glow and a grin.

"How was your tram?" I asked.

"Direct and efficient, Casaubon." He paused and looked around. "It is nice up here. I can understand why you might enjoy doing your exercises here. I have spent some time here attending rituals. Such a range of gods, pantheons, and mythos, and ha, even book clubs meet here. It is not all Sacred. There is beautiful Profane that is associated with this place and a place like this. More on that later. This place has been on my mind since I was relayed your call. But first we must work."

"Yes, of course. Work. The call. We are here. To meet with. An avatar for a mountain goddess," I replied.

"Exactly, Casaubon. The goddess, Dayang Masalanta, and she's right over there."

Changes

The call had come in today, Friday, August 25, 2220, at noon precisely. Since it was not an emergency, but a missing person, I was able to take some notes after, alert Thinkowitz, and we both made it here at one o'clock.

The call had come from his sister; she was worried about her brother as he never came home last night. She was sweet, and there was a true sincerity to her worry. She had sent him a Buzz. It was confirmed as received, but he has yet to reply.

His name is 'Aho'eitu "Momo" Latu, and he worships the Tongan goddess, Hikule'o, the Goddess of the Underworld, known as Pulotu.

Sione Latu, the sister, twenty years old, told me, "Momo

is a nickname. It means 'crumb.' It is kinda fun and mean, I guess, but affectionate. My brother worships Hikuleʻo, and I worship Seketoa, like duh. Great white shark fish god is so cool. And like so Tongan. Our whole family worships from the Tongan pantheon, but our parents worship really esoteric gods in the pantheon, practically very localized woodland demi-gods or spirits.

"They were of that generation. You know, *the more out there, but still in there, the better*. That way of thinking. Very City. But it was out of pride. You know. Proud enough to do work. To study up. To dig deep. Old days stuff. That was before they moved here to Tucker. It's not the suburbs, but still.

"So to them it does feel a little sad about Momo, uhm, I mean ʻAhoʻeitu, to want to switch gods out of pantheon, but they accept it. It's his choice. They're happy for him. They want him to be happy.

"But that's the thing. He's in love. He says he's in love. He's in love with a goddess, an avatar of a goddess who he wants to worship. That kind of harmony of emotional, sexual, and spiritual in energy and focus should be encouraged. Right? You know?

"The thing is he's just so confused. He wouldn't admit it, but I can see it. He's my little brother, I know him. He's eighteen, and you know, going through changes.

"He says he's drawn to her like the moon. I don't get it.

—

She's not even a moon goddess, she's a mountain goddess. I guess they are both like round white rocks though. It is cool to look up at the moon from the top of New Gibraltar. It's all kinda the opposite of the underworld, but that's the deity he chose when he was fourteen. He thought it was pretty cool back then. And now he is eighteen, and thinks he knows everything. He's been going to EDF's a lot. I used to go to those more. But he is newly into the whole Ego Death Fest thing. 'Tis the season, though, right, and the 27th is just coming up.

"I'm just worried and scared. I woke up like this. With this feeling. This foreboding. And I waited all morning for him. It is totally strange for him to not come home. He's so mopey. He's either here, or spying on her, or dancing and losing himself to music and movement. He wouldn't be anywhere else.

"I know he went to talk to her last night. I think to like tell her. Like that he loved her and everything. That he wanted to worship her. And now he's gone. I think it might be Sacred. His disappearance. There are things I've heard about her that make me think there is something Sacred about him not coming home."

Sione told me her birth name is Maria Makiling, and she comes from a Filipino pantheon community in New Gibraltar. She has spent her whole life all over that rock, exploring every inch of its cracks and crags and arboreal ring.

When she turned twenty-five, she took on the avatarship of Dayang Masalanta, the goddess she was raised to venerate, after seven years of direct training in her community. The training was focused on mythology, botany, geology, and acts of service. She also took that new name in veneration of goddess she sought to embody.

In my quick research, Dayang Masalanta was a spirit or goddess of Mount Makiling, which was once a stratovolcano in Laguna, Philippines. Dayang Masalanta had power over deluges, storms, and earthquakes. There were several stories of missing or ill-fated lovers who haunted her woodlands and mountain.

She Gazed a Gazely Stare

I looked to where he pointed and there across the uneven summit, bald and pocked, still amid the back and forth cutting flow of visitors was a radiant woman crouched and bent over a dark puddle.

She wore a white, silken shift. A shimmering white light on almost black flesh, shimmering in its own darkness. She shined under the mid-day sun beating down through the Dome, a sparkle against pallid rock and murky fluids.

Walking towards her it became clear that she was staring down into the waters rippled gently by the breeze. She looked beyond the ripples.

"Hello, are you Dayang Masalanta?" asked my partner.

As she didn't reply, he added, "I'm Sacred Detective Rabbi Rabbinowitz, and this is my partner, Assistant Sacred Detective Edwina Casaubon."

"More like fairies than monkey." She spoke still bent, crouched, and gazing into the calming murk.

We paused waiting for clarity.

"The shrimp!" she said, rising to a height above mine at five four, and almost to that of Thinkowitz at six two.

Standing there before me on the other side of the little rock pock pond, it was hard not to compare myself to this woman. I had suspicions as to what might have drawn 'Aho'eitu to her.

Her body looked strong, like I hone mine to be. And yet, there was a pure-joy innocence radiating from her; less familiar to me. And then also something sexual surging in a compellingly feminine way. Something I only occasionally attempt to embody for myself and others. With her it seemed natural and powerful. Here she was on a Friday afternoon, maybe idly on top of this rock, maybe with purpose I've yet to learn, peering down into a puddle and radiating strength, joy, femininity while exuding smells of the earth and dirt and the tangy-tartness of sweet-sweat. I could feel the New Moon coming on Tuesday, the 29th.

She wore nothing beneath the shimmery shift. The freeness of her body in this breeze drew mine as I imagined it would draw anyone's. I understood deeply what drew 'Aitu'eitu. She was an avatar. Was this what a goddess is like? I had met several avatars, of always differing levels of intensity, of commitment. Is that what draws us, the intensity of commitment?

"I've been spending time, as of late, in our Archives, amusing myself in the secular, cultural productions of the past. The oddest little product caught my eye and interest. For a few decades in the middle of the 20th century, in a pre-digital period, tiny little eggs, dormant and dry in cryptobiosis, were sent directly to people who wanted to possess them and gestate them.

"The tiny little eggs hatched a tiny creature they called a Sea Monkey."

Her speaking brought me out of my rapt revelry. She had seemed not to notice, so I nonetheless modulated to give attention to anything else. But in this she somehow caught me.

"You're right, Edwina. There *should* be a pylon there. I would embrace it. The Mountain longs to serve. And I am sure we could still protect these little ones," Dayang Masalanta said.

I couldn't speak immediately. I couldn't face that feeling of being so known from the outside. I caught myself before a stammer. I couldn't stop what felt like an audible gulp. And in that moment, doubt crept in. The words of the sister, Sione, *there are things about her*, and then the myths, *ill-fated lovers*.

"Ah, yes, the fairy shrimp. I'm sure, Dayang Masalanta, that they would always be protected. They have endured so much." My partner cut in almost protectively of me, leading the conversation, and our investigation. "Have you seen them, Casaubon? This is their season. They have continued here for centuries before the Katastrophe and in their process of cryptobiosis where they hide dry in these cracks have endured the worst of the world before the Dome. Now in this arranged wet season of ours, they are reactivated, back to life in these little pools."

I observed the still shallow pool, a large puddle cut by our three shadows. The little fairy shrimp, Sea Monkeys, she said they were once called, flitted about. Thinkowitz retained control of our interaction.

"We are here to speak with you about a young man named, 'Aho'eitu. He never came home last night, and his sister is worried about him. She thought that you might have seen him. That he might have visited you last night," Sacred Detective Rabbinowitz asked.

She clasped her hands at her wide waist and stood

calmly before us.

"Yes, I know this young man. And yes, he came to see me officially for the first time last evening here. I say officially because I have felt his eyes upon me grazing, glancing, and even battering upon my flesh. I know the effects I can have, but he was being rude; though I understood this to be mostly confusion with no malign yearnings.

"I told him that he confused his lust with devotion. And that he should worship out of a purer spiritual motive. My words were stern, but not mean. He nodded in understanding and held back tears. He was wearing a touch-up jump suit, touched-up to the image color of this mountain. Of my Makiling. It was a sweet gesture. Come with me," she said and started walking west.

We followed a few steps behind her. My attention fell to her bare feet as her toes gripped and held and then sprung off of every corner and ridge of rock. It was like they were reading and sculpting the landscape at once.

She led us to the edge of the summit at a path down just a little south-west of the one I traversed to get up here. She pointed at a very specific and narrow path down through the arboreal ring, and then at a great wide low building at the edge of the woods bordering the rising buildings of New Gibraltar. The roof of the building appeared to be double-sided touch glass similar to that used in the Dome.

"That is where he went. That is the Temple of Ninshubur Gardens. It is a greenhouse of wild bio-diversity. Some of the seeds were from all the way in Svalbard. In the evenings the space hosts Ego Death Fests. When I realized where he was heading, it confirmed my suspicions that he was in a transitional space. I know nothing more. I do hope he is safe, and I hope he comes out of whatever transitional phase he is going through with new clarity," she said as she backed away slowly.

Thinkowitz gave her a short bow and nod, his eyes lowering briefly, and then she was gone, over the edge and around a sharp ridge to the steep south side of New Gibraltar. She moved like no human I'd ever seen. The grace was bestial.

"Gentleness is true strength," said my partner.

Now he seemed to be reading my mind.

"My father used to tell me that when I was a little girl," I replied.

"It was essential Profane Wisdom of the RESURGA. I see her strength in you, Casaubon. Dayang. Don't let the avatar-status fool you. She's still a human being. She just has a different kind of training. We are what we make ourselves. Her magic was simply catching your furtive glance at the nearest pylon and then the empty space at the center of the summit."

And then he walked slowly and carefully down, and I followed. Caught up, I walked alongside my partner.

Evergreens

We were greeted at the wide glass doors, polarized and oily to the eye. The whole, wide, rectangular facility was just a chrome frame around panels of this glass. Its placement demarcated the boundary between the mountain park of New Gibraltar and the neighborhood of New Gibraltar that starts at the opposite western entrance to us and continues down Bayard Rustin Avenue.

Our greeter was the priestess of this temple, Jojo Lee. She cracked the doors and invited us in. Then she stepped back a few paces giving us space to take it all in. There were waist-high beds of greens, and yellows, and oranges as far as the eye could see, fifty yards at the longest, thirty at the widest. A labyrinthian footpath was arranged through the beds with eddies in all directions. A web of irrigation spray pipes hung above our heads.

On the way here, through the woods, Thinkowitz explained to me that The Temple of Ninshubur was originally in Akkil, in ancient Sumeria, in the empire of Ur. Ninshubur was a lower goddess in the service of Inanna. She was integral in bringing Inanna back to life after she went to the underworld.

This facility nurtured and grew as starts a wide variety of plants and crops from all over the Pre-Katastrophe globe in a controlled environment. These *starts* were eventually moved to the fields of the I-285 and I-20 greenways. Other cultivation facilities, some stacked high in towering buildings, all benefitted from the initial work here. Plants that found their start here included: squash, maize, dragon fruit, ginseng, and chrysanthemum.

As we explored the space with our eyes, and I traced my fingers down the fuzzy leave of a nearby watermelon plant, Jojo Lee spoke first. She was a guide here; this was her temple.

Small and sallow, her skin was greyish like the milk we make from oats. Her hair poofed up and out, gray and yellow. Her smile was sincere and there was a wizened joy in her eyes, cradled in deep wrinkles. She wore white work pants of cotton fiber, and a matching shirt. Over both was an apron embroidered with vines. She had on yellow work gloves.

"I do this work in part as penance, and the performance of my duties are a lament. The original town of this temple, Akkil, its name means lament. That is why I worship Ninshubur, since her great work was in retrieving our lost love, our lost goddess of love, and oh so many things," she said, beaming with subtle crone power.

"Why do you have Ego Death Fests here? Is that in preparation for the upcoming Profane Holiday? How does the music and all the movement affect the plants?" I asked.

"I was approached a few months ago initially by a group of worshippers of various purgation and intoxication deities. They were establishing pop-up Ego Death Fests around in different neighborhoods. It was an effort to help people unfamiliar with the practice to connect for the first time before *The Great Day of Mourning* this year. They showed me these Shared-Audio-Experience-Sensor stickers," she said as she drew out from her apron a circle of thin, white, ribbed carbon fiber about the size of my thumb nail.

"They stick behind your ears, and everyone inside this Temple can share the same music silently. The plants hear not sound, but they seem to enjoy the movement and energy and sweat and moisture," she continued.

Then she showed us how the beds of soil, fecund and

overflowing with greens of leaves, and limbs, and vines, rolled on wheels and moved to the sides and in different patterns of the wide and airy space for the EDF evenings.

I unfolded a touch-tablet from the breast pocket on my jumpsuit and pulled up the photo of 'Aho'eitu his sister sent me and showed it to the priestess of the temple to ask if she saw him last night and can confirm his presence.

"Ha!" She delighted. "I thought it would be unlikely. And it was unlikely. There were over two thousand people here last night. But unlikely things happen. I did see him. It was towards the end of the night. Around four o'clock. He left through the south entrance with a local boy, from New Gibraltar, Anurak."

"Anurak Phonsavanh, the son of Lamon Phonsavanh?" asked my partner.

"Why yes! Do you know Lamon?"

"I do. Yes. My gentle friend. Thank you for your help, Priestess Jojo Lee. We are all grateful for the work you do here. Casaubon, do you have any further questions?"

"You stay until the end of the night at Ego Death Fests?" I asked her. It was hard to imagine this sweet, small woman who reminded me of the faint memories I have of my grandmother dancing at an Ego Death Fest that late.

"Why yes! I never leave these plants unattended. My home is attached. But I also like to watch the dancing. I choose to leave the SAES off and watch the movements in silence. The contortions and undulations of the human body has the potential of infinite creativity. As the ego dies, patterns break free to chaos. I watch people lose themselves, and I pray they rebuild stronger."

I went to shake her hand and she hugged me. She was smaller than me, but her reach was mysteriously encompassing. Thinkowitz stood aside and smiled softly and might have been stifling a bit of a laugh.

"Allow the prayer of this place to follow you," Jojo Lee said, as I broke our embrace and moved with my partner.

She raised her hands and spoke, "Go from this House of Mighty Eyes. This Temple of Ninshubur Gardens. I invoke you! From your heart flows wealth. Your vault is a mountain of abundance, and your sweet smell is a mountain of grapevines. Your righteous steward is foremost in heaven. Ninshubur. May she guide you."

Boy Likes to Dance

Leaving through the western exit, we walked from that green dream out down Bayard Rustin Avenue into the undeniable City. It is all around, while the almost exclusive naturality of New Gibraltar and environs can for a moment make us forget our world.

The Dome, and therefore the pylons and buildings, might be lower out in the suburbs where my parents live, where I lived while in Profane Safety before my transfer to Sacred, but the state of our world is inescapable. The nights that I walk and explore the I-285 Greenway I let my fingertips drag along the leaves of crops and cover. The life within supports my life within.

For our last case, my first in Sacred, the thickness and energy of life in the City was an awakening experience for me. It's something I continued to revel in awe of as I explored and familiarized further.

Walking into the neighborhood of New Gibraltar, the town around the western side of rock, the greens and yellows and ochers and oranges of the organic were projected by *us* back to us on the touch-up walls of the towering buildings. The details eased acclimation for those of us who truly give themselves over to enjoying the Temple of Ninshubur Gardens and the arbor ring at the base of New Gibraltar.

Due to the proximity of the rock, the town drew communities of formerly island dwelling traditions, and formerly coastal traditions of Southeast Asia in particular.

The touched-up fabric of the clothes of those who passed us illustrated the will to keep the feel of nature with us and for others. Many of the people I've come to know this past year have names in reference to flowers and the natural world. A tool is a tool. There is no irony for us that we use our technologies to emulate nature. We use our technologies to preserve nature, and what is natural about ourselves. That is part of life Post-Katastrophe, Post-Kapital-death. No technology is for its own sake. It is all for ours, for the Greater Good.

Being for us, our technologies are also used for pleasure, enjoyment, and aesthetics, key components of life. It was less than a mile into New Gibraltar, and one block off the main avenue, before we stood in front of a five-story pink frog of a building, eyes-bulging, jaw set as if to *kero kero*, snug in a cracked alley between two older, duller towering buildings.

"This, Casaubon, is the home of Lamon Phonsavanh. He built it himself over a great many years. It is modeled on a lost building from some centuries ago he learned of in our Archive. Lamon worships Phraya Khan Kaka, the Toad King of Thailand. He worships a god for this season, Casaubon. The Toad King brought the rains."

"Does he live here to be close to the greenhouse as well as the rock?" I asked.

"Yes. But he also has his own accommodations within. Come." He knocked and then immediately opened the door at the lighter-pink, lower abdomen of the frog.

We entered into a great round hall, which at its center rose up to a rotunda five stories high. Subtle sounds of *keros* and chirps permeated the space within the sounds of running water. The interior rooms were all built up around the inner walls, a spiral staircase wrapping around the interior space and connecting each level. From the center ceiling of the rotunda, water fell like dense rains, down the middle of the five stories until the floor absorbed it, never allowing pooling.

The house was filled with voices and all the noises of domestic life. The words I could make out through the bluster hinted towards knowledge of our presence. Soon, an older man, about forty-five years old glided to us in soft, satin slippers and a long red robe, its pattern a mixture of hand-embroidered pink frogs holding rainbow umbrellas, and touch-up panels above each with video clips of rain pouring down.

His hair was straight and black, parted in the middle back behind his ears, with the two ends pulled forward over each shoulder and braided with the corresponding half of his long straight black beard also parted in the middle. His skin was a rich tawny-tan slightly darker than my own.

"Ah, welcome, Rabbi. Welcome, welcome, my friend! Is this your partner I've heard about? Hello, Assistant Detective," greeted Lamon Phonsavanh.

I returned his greeting, and we shook hands and did a low, smiling bow. I always felt such immediate affection from friends of Thinkowitz, of whom there are many.

"Thank you for this visit. Shall I make tea? Shall we sit? We could sit dry over on the couches, or wet around the rains?"

"I am sorry to tease with the notion of a social visit, Lamon," said Thinkowitz. "We are here on business, hopefully not unfortunate business, but we do not know yet. Your eldest son might have information that can help us."

—
29

"Anurak, my little angel? He is around here somewhere. Probably still asleep. Or back asleep. I heard him earlier. He was out very late. Oh wait, there he is," said Lamon.

Over the railing separating the fifth floor from the open center was thrown a weighted rope-ladder. Over the railing and onto the rope-ladder climbed a man who appeared to be a younger version of Lamon Phonsavanh. And without the facial hair.

He climbed down slowly and dramatically, a performance for our pleasure of the rope-ladder swinging almost uncontrollably and then steadied. With purpose, but no practical reason, the climber switched sides of the ladder as if describing a spiral of his own making. By the time he reached the bottom rung, he had been back up to the middle of the ladder and down almost to the end twice. He moved as if there was a music that only he could hear. Likely, a silly music.

"Anurak, come say hello to the Rabbi, and meet his partner, Assistant Detective Edwina Casaubon," said Lamon Phonsavanh. "The Rabbi says you might have information that can help an investigation. I will get tea."

The young man, who up close looked even more like a younger version of his father, but with a simpler style of clothing: two-piece pajamas patterned with pink monkeys at play. I noted that he was twenty years old.

We sat in the "dry area" on couches of slick vegetable-vinyl upholstery. I imagined the couches could withstand being closer to the wet area if needed.

Sacred Detective Rabbinowitz silently allowed me to lead, and I showed Anurak the image of 'Aho'eitu and related that Priestess Lee observed them leaving together last night.

"Oh yeah, totally. Momo. I know him, and I saw him last night. I don't know him well. It was, I guess, the second time we've met, last night. We did leave together. Yes, that is true. But that might be the most of the story."

"What do you mean?" I asked.

"I love to dance. And I really go for it. I just let myself go. Really. A lot. And I'm all over the space. And it's EDF's all the time. Sometimes I use intoxicants to really help drive that ego death feeling home. But not last night, I'm saving that for Sunday, for the holiday. I worship Hanuman, the Monkey God. He's a trickster, but I'm more about movement, and play, and silliness. Those aspects of the god.

"Last night I was happy to run into Momo again. We are similar how like he also just likes to let himself go in dance, and really be all over the place. We got to know each other a week or so ago at a different EDF since we just kept passing each other in weird places around the space. He really likes the intoxicants though. I think it's mostly the psilocybin cookies. Last night he was kinda the same, but also mopier, and then would be like energized, and then looked really sad. He was all over the place, but in a different way, you know. I definitely saw him eat some of the cookies.

"At the end of the night I was really wiped out. Like wiped. Momo was all sweaty like me, and his eyes were red, and kinda wild looking. But that's not that weird at an EDF. We were at the south end of Temple, that's where we just both kinda rested. And yeah, the priestess was there. I told Momo, *I really need to go home*. And he said, *ok*, and we walked out the south exit together."

Lamon Phonsavanh refilled our tea. I held my cup out with one hand and the unfolded tablet with the other to record Anurak's account. He continued after a shared sip of tea.

"I thought he said 'ok' because he was accepting my invitation to come home with me for the night. I know he lives in Tucker and my house was a much closer walk. Until you both came here and asked questions, I thought he was lucky he didn't come with me."

"Why? What happened last night?" I asked.

"Well, so, we walked right out that exit. The south exit. And I've never left the Temple that way. The western exit is a straight shot to my house. But this way let us out into the woods. There were trails, but it was dark under the tree branches, and I had no idea where to go. The tree cover was so dark I couldn't even see the glow of New Gibraltar town. I stumbled in one direction and looked back and Momo was gone. I called out, but he didn't answer. I couldn't see anything. My eyes weren't adjusting. I was so lost. It took me almost two hours to get home."

"That I can confirm, Detectives. I noted my son coming home at six o'clock, and wondered as to why he was later than normal," said Lamon.

"And you haven't heard from Momo today, Anurak?" I asked.

"Nah, I'm sorry. I've mostly just been asleep. It was a weird night. It was spooky in those woods. I have lots of weird scratches and insect bites. More ego death happened after I left the Fest. Ha."

We took one last sip of the tea, and then thanked the Phonsavanh family for such a welcome and the information.

We walked out of the lower abdomen of the giant pink frog house, knowing more, and now with new knowledge, knowing how little we really knew. We were on Fourth Street between Bayard Rustin Avenue and Mountain Avenue.

I was about to ask my partner how he knew Lamon Phonsavanh, but he spoke first.

"Detective Casaubon, allow us to continue to do our due diligence of investigation with the next step left to us. Let us work through negative deduction, rule options out, and narrow search parameters." He had stopped in the middle of the street while saying this and then led me to the closest building wall. While we—or at least I— generally have the necessary technologies on our person, they are always at-hand as most surfaces are designed with touch-up capabilities, and connection to our Archives and the shared Digital Public Forum.

There was a tea lounge and a grocery center on the bottom floor of the building we stopped at. Above were apartments, communal living quarters, and other spaces for active and creative engagement, like most buildings in the City. The closest guests in the tea lounge smiled and waved at us. They seemed to know my partner.

He acknowledged, and at the corner of the window, away from obstructing any view, he tapped and then touched-up access to City Archives and the Digital Public Forum. Everything from the Digital Public Forum, all updates and statuses on citizen life and living, all information is also printed and stored in a Material Public Forum, which is then stored at City Hall.

Sacred Detective Rabbinowitz connected to the BDMS, the Breath/Death Monitoring System. No change was recorded in the last twenty-four hours. The last change in Breath-Content within the Dome was documented as a death two days ago. The certainty of this Monitoring System is ninety-eight percent. This room of error is assumed as a comfort since we are collectively essentially frightened of dogma, and some doubt must always be allowed on practice. Our collective trauma extends into deep and varied realms.

Wherever 'Aho'eitu Latu was, at least he was still breathing. This is a positive development. This gives us and his family hope. But we need more than hope. He was last seen in the woods of the arboreal ring around New Gibraltar mountain, near the south exit/entrance of The Temple of Ninshubur Gardens. We should head there next, and have Profane Investigators sent to help search.

I was about to state this obvious next step as my partner was tapping-out of the touched-up glass accessing the BDMS, and then everything changed.

We know that coincidence is a matter of attention, not magic, that the inexplicable is something that has *yet* to be explained, like Dayang Masalanta interpreting my movements earlier, not actually reading my mind; but here it was, a confluence of alarms and warnings, notifications, all at once, to both of us out of our personal communications—buzzed on our wristwatches —and there on the wall in the Digital Public Forum, the program aware of Thinkowitz in use.

There's been a murder, in a Sacred situation, in a very different part of town.

Blood, Blood, Blood

The most direct tram from New Gibraltar got us to the West End fast, and the elevator down the pylon let us out a block from what had recently become known as the Avatar Arts District. En route we made the call to send searchers into the woods to look for 'Aho'eitu.

Traditionally the West End, around the intersection of Ralph David Abernathy Boulevard and Lawton Street, has been a neighborhood where people share very refined and formal art forms in various galleries, and other meeting places of personal, creative development have risen in the area. Clinics and facilities for avatar-training have increased over the last few years. The store fronts down Ralph Abernathy Boulevard west towards Langhorne Street now bare several signs that read "Integrative Avataring," "Actualized Avatar Training,"

"Deification Station," and other such conceptual combinations.

The phenomenon has confused and excited me since the first avatars I met on my debut case with Thinkowitz. Avatar therapy developing in practice in this neighbor is even more confusing for me, but makes sense in that some people—many apparently—see the act of avataring as a performance art, a Sacred practice of performance art. From what I understand, avataring is aspirational, it is a process, and it is never complete. It is the height of mysticism.

This is the worst way to enter an avatar therapy practice for an initial visit, and I was terrified at what we would find. More terrified than I had ever been.

Citizens passing-by gave a respectful wide berth around the entrance as we walked up. Faces were tearful and concerned, and clothing that had most likely been touched-up with color and image, was now dim and reverent.

At the front door to the therapy space, the bottom floor of a very tall and ornate tower of a building, waited the proprietor in partnership under a sign that read "Mystical Embrace." She appeared shut down within herself—grief-held—while standing upright, with the doorway as subtle support. My partner went to comfort her, and they embraced. She wore a carbon-fiber, complete touch gown, black like a shroud from neck to ground, an impossible, electric black. Her long hair in tight black curls fell around her shoulders. Her face was long and narrow, with a sharp, downward nose, and narrow, cat-like eyes. Her skin was olive with cream.

"Edwina Casaubon, this is Lisa-Marie Sicily, she is one of the pioneers in avatar-training, and her clinic here is one of the oldest in operation. She no longer lives as an avatar, but she worships the Roman goddess, Cardea, a goddess of hinges and handles. It is a name that translates as 'door-pivot.' As a devotee, Lisa-Maria is a caretaker of liminal spaces, and she facilitates transitions. It took years of living as an avatar of that goddess for her to understand it on a pedagogical level."

He told me all of this, and I exchanged greetings with Lisa-Marie, as we moved with intention through the foyer of clinic down a long hall of white light to an open doorway where stood a City Safety Officer.

Lisa-Marie stopped at the threshold, not within it, but distinctly at it, and told us, "Pearl Iko was meeting with a new client. A walk-in. I was upstairs. I heard the bell, she didn't buzz up to me for assistance, so I continued what I was doing. This is a common occurrence for us both. Some people make appointments. Some wander in led by curiosity."

When it was clear that she wouldn't follow us into the room, the potential crime scene, we waited a moment as she left us with more explanation:

"Pearl Iko worships the Japanese goddess, Ama-terasu, a sun deity. She lived for two years as Ama-terasu's avatar before undergoing her pedagogical training with me. She is quite proficient at facilitating the avatar process. All of her several clients over the last year since she has been a lead facilitator have expressed satisfactory results. It is inconceivable to me as to how this could happen. I do not understand what I see in there. Sessions are one-on-one and based on trust. The first session begins the process of trust as much as connection with the deity."

My partner, Sacred Detective Rabbinowitz, and I entered the cube of a room. In the center was a seven-by-four-foot rectangle, a bed or an altar, raised to three feet off the floor and draped messily with a thick, white touch-blanket. Otherwise, the room was un-adorned. I watched my partner scan the space, and I trusted in his skills, but there wasn't much to work with.

"It's a touch-box. Just a fully-fitted touch-room with a touch-floor connected to the Digital Public Forum and Archive, and gesture controls set for both myself and Pearl. We apply diodes to the patient's temples to read the image waves when the guiding voice brings forth the desire to picture your deity. The control box for the diodes and the image-generation system are built into the wall just within the doorway to the right," Lisa-Marie spoke from the other side of the doorway as my partner and I spread out around the room to investigate.

On the other side of the center raised rectangle was the puddle. It was a subtle horror as it alluded to more than it showed. It was a lot of blood. More than I had ever seen alone in one place. Once charged with life, its spread was slowing, and it was settling into a low, rusty, amorphous blob. In the size and thickness, the horror lay.

"How does the process work in here?" I asked Lisa-Marie in an effort to take my mind off the focus before me.

"It is conception and conjuration at once. It is the first step—imagining—before eventually embodying. No transference can happen unless some form of physical contextualization does. And it must be explicit and bold. All-encompassing. That's step one. That's what having all surfaces of this room touched-up to images does. The client is surrounded, overcome, embattled, consumed, and devoured by the deity they worship. In this room, what is inside of them appears to come from outside. Step two is in the next room, a more comfortable room of total sensory-deprivation in which you wear a sensory-contained ocular headset and the body soaks in a thick plasma fluid. That step, and room, involve internal saturation."

We had so much more to go on in our last crime scene investigation. The altar and session room of Tiresias Pythia contained a body and signs of struggle. There were witnesses to question. Tiresias had a notable relation with a large public. They was loved and respected widely. There was nothing here, but a puddle of blood. We were here, because whatever happened happened in a Sacred situation. In sessions this becomes a hallowed ground.

Sacred Detective Rabbinowitz had stopped looking around and stared at the blood between us.

"What does the blood tell you?" I asked him.

"It tells me what it should tell you too, Casaubon." He squatted low and tilted his head, squinting, and drew back up.

"Look at the thickness and expanse of the shape," he instructed. "As a volume measurement, how much blood would you deduce here?"

I performed the same squat and tilt. I reorganized the liquid mass in my mind visually.

"My estimate is that there is approximately somewhere between three and a half to about four and a half quarts, around four quarts total."

"Lisa-Marie, I met Pearl Iko twice here while visiting you over the last year. The last time was two months ago. I found her to be five feet and two inches, a slight, narrow build."

Lisa-Marie nodded in approval at his description.

"Casaubon, if this is Pearl Iko's blood—and that test will be very easy and quick to determine as we are surrounded with touch surfaces with a connection to our Archives—do you think someone that size could continue to live without this much blood?

"No," I said sadly and seriously. "This is about the approximate average blood content for an adult human body, but without a body we cannot say definitively. Should we check the BDMS again?"

Thinkowitz moved the white touch blanket on the raised rectangle, a bed, a bench, an altar. On the flat surface he touched-up the Forum and connected to the BDMS and contrary to earlier, a change was now detected. One less breath registered for life in the dome; one less breath equals a death, a change in our equilibrium. All of the machinery that supports life for us and all other organisms in this Dome are calibrated in a delicate balance of human breath.

We looked at each other knowingly. Uncertainty and mystery still remained as to whether the new rate, and abatement of breath is from 'Aho'eitu Latu or Pearl Iko. Two missing people, one puddle of blood, one abated breath.
"You mentioned earlier that nothing like this has every happened before? This is a complete aberration?" I asked Lisa-Marie Sicily.

"Yes, nothing at all," said Lisa-Marie. "Results are most often favorable, with few exceptions where the client expresses dissatisfaction with an inability to connect with their deity. Or to feel a connection. A downturn of mood and dissatisfaction have been the worst results. Nothing like this. Nothing."

"The appearance here, and the details that you have given us indicate that something happened during the avataring session. Is there anything that you can think of to counter that supposition?" I asked, grounding our certainties and parsing out our mysteries. I was following Sacred Detective Rabbinowitz's methodologies of negative deduction—a process he adapted from Moses Maimonides, and taught at Safety Academy—making a clear delineation between our knowns and unknowns.

"So, if the act of violence occurred during her session with the client, maybe the god who was sought was a violent god, or a war god. Maybe the client identified with hostility inherent in that deity?" I asked.

"That would be something that I've never seen, but it could explain what happened. Pearl Iko is dedicated to finding all of her clients' supportive connections to their gods. She is... was... very good at her work. Our failures exist from ineffectiveness; we've never worried about being too effective. If this client connected with their deity to the level of violent expression, it would be like nothing I've ever seen. Nothing I thought possible.

A very powerful god. I hope and I pray that this is an accident. But an accident speaks to a new danger. This is not what I want for the practice of avataring," said Lisa-Marie emotionally, looking tired and worn, grief cutting jaggedly through the joy cracks at the edges of her eyes and mouth.

"If it was an accident, then where is she, or her body? Who could act like this without guilt, or through the guilt? I do not see, nor smell, any vomit in this space. What other explanations are there?" I reasoned out loud.

"Our collective guilt is mostly triggered by greed, Casaubon. I do see guilt here, or possibly a response to an accident that is understood to be socially inappropriate or abominable," cut-in my partner, taking the lead.

"Lisa-Marie, how many touch blankets are kept in this and the other first stage rooms on the altar?" he asked.

"It is always two. This room is meant to be less comfortable than the second immersive stage, but a top and bottom blanket add warmth and basic comforts for such a harsh and dynamic environment as this," she answered.

There was only one blanket. My mind was following the pattern of reason and narrative re-construction that my partner was leading it to.

"Maybe, if Casaubon's supposition is accurate, and the client identified with the hostility of the deity, the violence was one of spontaneity. It is not prudent to suppose, but what we do have here is the negative presence of a touch blanket, a blanket the same size as the one remaining on the altar, and therefore large enough to contain discretely the body of Pearl Iko after this quantity of blood has been let. The client, who must therefore be of significant strength, could—and what other option is there?—exit this building with Pearl wrapped in the touch blanket unbeknownst to any passersby. We shall leave an empty space in our running report for 'the why' since materially it matters less than 'the more-likely-how,' which we do have a clue towards," concluded the senior detective.

While I listened, I drew a secure swab from a pocket on my tactical jumpsuit, and after rolling it gently into the surface of the fading rust-colored puddle, I pressed it against the touch screen on the altar. The identity confirmation was instantaneous. I pointed this out to Thinkowitz, and he nodded in acknowledgement.

He took time to wander slowly around the room a little more. His brow grazed and glanced in sweeps and squints, but despite the blood, it was a clean room of touch-surfaces, an altar, and a touch-blanket.

"The images from the diodes attached to the client's head that are reflected back at them across these surfaces, they aren't recorded, correct?" he asked casually in the direction of Lisa-Marie.

"Correct. The images are as ephemeral as the whole experience for the seeker. It is not for us to keep a record of that," she replied.

"So only they know what they saw," he said, and trailed off, his furrowed brow cast in shadow beneath his low fedora. He started to pace, almost about to speak again in any moment, and then it passed, and then approached again.

Lisa-Maria and I passed small grins of comfort back and forth, but they fell flat under the weight of the situation and the anxiety his pacing churned up. Soon he stopped, and with a mild awareness of his impact. He put his hands on the outer shoulders of Lisa-Marie and spoke softly to her across the threshold. I lingered off to the side respectfully. Her large dark eyes welled-up with moisture, at the precipice of bursting.

We walked out of the room to her, then with her, and then at the foyer we passed by her out into the street.

"There is a killer on the loose, Casaubon," my partner said as soon as we were alone, back into the passing crowds of the West End. "Whoever they is, they is acting out of impulse and then self-preservation, but still killing. 'Aho'eitu might be related, but I fear there will be more killing."

He was moving swiftly with purpose, and I followed, listening. I didn't understand our direction or purpose until I realized the time. After two blocks we were at the tram stop and we took the lift up to a North-East directional tram. I stayed with him the whole way to Sandy Springs.

On the tram my partner continued in a didactic mode. We stood the whole way. He was deliberating out loud. It was clear that he did it for me, and that it was a slowed down version of his cognitive processes. He was breaking down what he experienced in his mind for a general audience with a normal brain, one without cyborg enhancements, one without an encyclopedic knowledge of world religious histories and traditions, one without instant access to its own saved memories and experiential knowledge.

I saw a puddle of blood where it shouldn't be, and a single touch-blanket where there should be two. Zero Peal Ikos where there should be one. I saw a pained Lisa-Marie Sicily where there should be a joyous one. I was starting to fear that my partner saw something that our world was, as-of-yet, unfamiliar with.

"The problem with certainty in an investigation is that we must rule out every single other possibility. Some things we can never know. Some things seem to not allow themselves to be known. Quite often the only certainty we have is partial, failed, flawed, incomplete, but it is the only truth that remains when everything else is ruled out. When working with mystery we must be comfortable with a lack of true certainty. This is all central in my approach to negative deduction," my partner continued.

"One cannot prove a negative, as you know, but one can find acceptance in mystery. We are not at that point yet here. There is more to know, and more that I believe we can ultimately know.

"With this investigation we have a compressed time-line, a very tidy and limited crime scene, but an uncertainty of motive and a lack of victim or body. We also have a missing person, a context not as clearly Sacred, and no obvious connection between the two cases. The only factual certainty is that we have less human breath in our air, a fact that gives evidence to a single death. This death could be 'Aho'eitu Latu, who never came home last night, or Pearl Iko who is missing from an avataring session, along with the client and a touch-blanket, but without a vital amount her own blood which was left behind.

"Please buzz City Safety to have photographs of both Latu and Iko displayed on the Digital Public Forum with a note to the public that both people are missing. I instructed Lisa-Marie Sicily to disseminate our concerns to the family and friends of Iko immediately so they will know of her disappearance and possible death, before you buzz City Safety. I put my trust in you, Casaubon. You have studied and trained for this," he concluded

—
49

exactly as the tram stopped and the doors slid open up above Sandy Springs.

Sacred Detective Rabbinowitz stepped off of the lift out onto the street a minute before six o'clock. I watched from above on the tram stop platform as he walked in the direction of his home at the beginning of his Sabbath.

Where Are We Now?

It was as if my partner laid out the cases before me with all of the conflicts and concerns for me to analyze, and then disappeared not to be seen for twenty-four hours. The disappearance was a weekly occasion, but has never left me with a case, let alone two cases, related or not.

I took the lift up the tram pylon to the next landing with a track in the direction of my apartment building in East Atlanta Village. I was heading home as a reflex; my partner concluded his workday so I did too. But this was like no other workday I've had before. And now on the tram heading southeast between Dome-supporting towers and pylons of stone and chrome, touch-glass and pressed carbon, I was experiencing feelings of unfamiliar unease.

The tram was almost full in the seating area around me. Families and friends laughed and talked and whenever they looked my way I tried to respond as politely as I could to the hellos and smiles and nods, but it was difficult. I positioned my head as if there was something out the window that was occupying my attention. But it was all a blur, and I let it be.

Buildings designed and ornamented with styles and flourishes from all over the world of human history. All different, all beautiful, all shared. And it was going by me in a blur. Something that usually excited me from just minimal attention. A blur.

I decided to wait a little longer before buzzing City Safety. That gave Lisa-Marie more time with Pearl Iko's family, but my delay stemmed more from a tension in myself between my reflex to relax, to physically and emotionally end my workday, and the fear that if I let go, if I take my mind off of all of this for just a moment something awful will happen again.

Thinkowitz had said, "A killer is on the loose."

It was an expression from ancient horror stories of the world before the Katastrophe, and examples of social control and fearmongering. But my partner wouldn't express this if he didn't think it was true, and he wouldn't say it in this contextual, referential way.

Our world has risen and stands on Somber-Hope. RESURGA is our motto. We are the inheritors of epigenetic markers of collective trauma resulting from the previously-inconceivable horrors we have witnessed and the nausea it brings. Risings seas and temperatures that steam breath from within. Billions dead. Civilizations and whole geographies gone. The Earth unlivable outside of a Dome.

The two closest children near me on the tram giggled and leap-frogged each other in the aisle. Their parents laughed. I looked away from the window and shared a smile with them, and then returned my attention to the blur.

Our world is not perfect. I hope that the time in which you live, Dear Future, is better, that you have learned from us, and our mistakes. I do not want to reduce or damage those smiles and moments of laughter and joy happening right around me with fear and the worry of a new danger.

The tram passed through Midtown, and I estimated that I still had time in a few minutes, before my stop, to follow the instructions of my partner. It was something I could do. Something helpful. The next step.

I was having a hard time keeping all these thoughts and feelings in particular inside. It was difficult to remain professional, rational, and protected against fears and doubts. Anyone could be this killer and this killer could be anywhere. My role in this society wasn't just to investigate things that have happened that might threaten our Sacred Safety, but to prevent a Sacred danger if possible. This is the clearest expression of that agenda.

My muscles started to flare, to ache. My stop was coming up, and I just wanted to be home. I had run so hard this morning. It had felt so good. And now I was feeling so weak. It felt like my footing was off. Like my guard was down, but somewhere that I couldn't reach. It started with her. The way she saw right through me. The way she read my mind by reading my movements. Dayang Masalanta. The reality was more intriguing than the illusion.

And then I saw my stop in the distance, a pylon directly in front of my building, and I drew out my touch-tablet for one last work task of the day before I can rest.

Unwashed and Somewhat Slightly Dazed

The elevator door of my building opened onto my floor and instantly I was startled with a loud—"BLAAHRRG"—a tongue thrust out and wagging, and presented:

Red hairs, a flaming pelt, crimsons, carmine, cerise, bursting woven with oranges, yellows, blondes, and ginger wire tresses, a thatched mat spread out across a downward triangle of vulva, out onto thigh-tops and a low tummy roll. Two little pink tabs puckered out from the center like two lips making a raspberry.

I shouted in surprise—a shriek—and then I buckled in laughter, deep, choking, uncontrollable laughter, and then tears broke through like a flood and as they poured down my body followed that trajectory. I crumpled on the floor, just inside from the doors of the lift. Erin Aspen released the hem of her green dress and lowered instantly to hold me in support and comfort. She squatted and clutched me up against her knee with my head on her bosom.

I cried and laughed, wrenchingly, messily, and she slowly rocked me and pressed my head against her.

The laughter gave way to tears that flowed freely.

Erin Aspen worshipped Baubo and had received consent from all of us who lived on this floor of the building to practice freely. Baubo was a Greek goddess of laughter, sacred healing, motherhood, and childcare. We had spent eight months since I moved here getting to know each other, talking, sharing meals, and building community with the other floormates and building-mates. This was the first time I had experienced her work when the initial response of laughter gave way to catharsis.

After a break in my tearful torrent, when I caught my breath and felt like I was sinking lower into Erin's bosom she sighed with me, expressing a deep breath, and then she lifted me up in her arms and carried me to my apartment. She took me straight to my bed, and as she laid me down it must have been clear what I needed.

She tucked me in, kissed my forehead, and smiled as she drew back, away. I remember her smile, and then I must have fallen asleep immediately.

In the morning my head was thick, and I felt slightly dehydrated. It had been a deep sleep with anxious, desperate dreams. I was grateful it was not *the* Dream, the expression of our collective trauma from the horrors of Kapital, but instead I experienced a dissonant and discordant montage of images and clips. It was as if my challenged mind was shaking off shards of memory and day residue. Shaking them off and scattering them about.

What I saw was the Dome; and the mountain, the rock, so white, a frightening white; and Goddess Nut, her pregnant belly glinting with power while she stood at the Dome edge in Griffin when I encountered her after we solved the death of the cyborg oracle; Dayang Masalanta's wide hips, the way they swung and shifted her tummy with each step, a shimmer of flesh like a small Dome-quake, the kind that for scale would trigger *the* Dream in most of us, but there was hope in those dark hips; and I saw the Dome from outside, above, and it made me feel so alone, and powerful, and totally free, but sad, and I woke up saying no to the sadness.

I was sore—physically, mentally, and emotionally—but it was an earned soreness that radiated with energy. It was the kind of soreness that powers me.

I woke up in my underwear. Erin Aspen had removed

my tactical jumpsuit and folded it onto the chair at the table in my apartment. I cherished her friendship, neighborliness, and praxis of worship. Baubo was such a wonderful figure to cut in a goddess, and it is so horrible to think how humans were at another time, a time long before the Katastrophe, who could marginalize towards wiping out her presence and influence, and physically harming her worshippers.

Baubo was said to transmit Sacred, feminine, healing energy simply by making someone laugh; by bringing on a big hearty belly laugh she was said to heal spiritual and emotional trauma. I understood what drew my friend to her calling.

Up, I adjusted the touch-tint setting to "clear" on the wall of windows that faced out from my apartment. I couldn't see to New Gibraltar around all the towers and pylons, but I loved to be able to look down on the green space of I-20 park that cut across the center of the City. I could touch-up the walls to be any image or video clip that we have in the Archives, and no matter how crisp that image can be, it can never compare with that real, living, breathing, greenness down below.

Sitting at the table by the window wall, I had my morning tea. At night I usually prefer Cubby Wubby Womb Room, a blend of soothing, comforting herbs mixed with green tea leaves. St. John's Wort, Fever Few, Valerian, and Lavender on an Oolong base. It is good for relaxing my mind and retainment as I read in evenings spent alone and home. In mornings, I wake my mind and body with a spicy chai blend in black tea. It was six o'clock when I woke, dawn for this season, and I liked to have my tea and feel my mind rouse while I looked out at the world around and below also rousing. There were twelve hours until I would see Thinkowitz again. It was a lot of time, and I could use it well.

I made a hearty and delightful porridge of oats and spelt grains with collard greens and soy sauce. I also set out for myself a bowl of blueberries that I continued to pick at after the porridge was finished. My work was beginning for the day right there at the table by my window-wall eating blueberries. Framed photos of my parents sat at the far end of the table and their sweet faces looked at me approvingly. Three low stacks of books framed the table tidily, the way that made me comfortable.

I checked the message board for City Safety Sacred Division and the Profane Officers had left a report that their search of the arboreal ring around New Gibraltar offered no traces of 'Aho'eitu Latu, nor did their expanded search which included the whole mountain itself. There were no other new messages regarding either case.

A new day, but still no 'Aho'eitu Latu and still no sighting of Pearl Iko, or her body. Was this a discreet killing, and therefore personal, or was it an act against avatars and avataring? Would this then involve 'Aho'eitu since he was in love with, and spurned by, a goddess avatar? Although we are all connected, coincidences happen around phenomena that are not directly related. Life is beautiful in its randomness. Mostly. Even if what happened to Pearl Iko was initially an accident, my partner sees something else. *There is a killer on the loose*. That implies that he thinks there will be more killing, or maybe at least that 'Aho'eitu is also a victim.

It was too much to manage with so little. I could make no connections. The details were like sand through my fingers. I tried to hold onto them, and there was nothing there, they just scattered into fragments under the minimum of pressure. I felt generally confident in myself, but alone with this case knowing that it would be half a day before I see Thinkowitz again. I needed him, but he had his traditions. I wasn't the only one who needed him. If he could understand these crimes in a way that no one else could then weren't his traditions standing in the way of the Greater Good? This weekend especially, I felt this need more than ever. A killer on the loose and tomorrow being what it is…

Dear Future, maybe you have healed, maybe you have moved on, but we still observe the Profane Holiday of *The Great Day of Mourning*. The following day, Sunday, August 28, was the celebration. Yes, on this day of mourning we celebrate. There are festivals and parties across our Domed-world, from out in the suburbs to the highest levels of tower-life in the City.

We glory and revel in being alive; even within our more somber and sullen tones. We revel in surviving, in spite of how committed we were to our own destruction. And on *The Great Day of Mourning* we let it all come out. Our pain, our sorrow, our grief, and then our great guilty relief.

This would be my first celebration of this great Profane holiday since living here, in the City. Instead of my usual Sunday morning visit to my parents' house out in the suburbs of Roswell, for our private family veneration of our Christ, had supposed I would enjoy the day, give over to the experience. And experience a greater closeness with my floor neighbors in the building. Maybe visit Uco Azul who I met on my first case with Sacred, and who I occasionally visit to enjoy the pulque he makes and the way his physical body feels and makes mine feel. However. Whatever vague plans I had formulated from before yesterday seemed so long ago at this time.

But I needed to do something. Something more than sit here. I couldn't just wait for my partner. I reviewed all the details of both cases on reflex in rotation in my mind, and there wasn't that much. If this is Sacred, then maybe the mystery lies in myth.

From the corner of my table looking out over I-20 and then into, and around, the towers, pylons and skyscrapers, I drew the top volume from a stack of books.

It was *The Guide for the Perplexed*, by Moses Maimonides, as I was trying to understand Thinkowitz better, and to be reading it made me feel like I was reading directly from his mind, but in an almost ancient style of writing.

In the second chapter of book one, Maimonides wrote as a retort, *Stay and think, for the matter is not as it appears to you at first blush, but as will emerge when we give our full consideration to the passage. The intellect which God bestowed on man as his ultimate perfection was the one which was given to Adam before his disobedience. It is that one which is meant by saying that Adam was made in the image and likeness of God.*

It sounded like something he might say, and also like something about him. After what the SunSpot Cyborg Program had done to and for him, there was something that felt almost god-like about my partner.

Yesterday, after the call from 'Aho'eitu "Momo" Latu's sister, Sione, I drew a volume of Filipino mythos from our library at Sacred Safety and gave the chapters on Dayang Masalanta a quick peruse. And there the book remained when I left to meet my partner.

Resolved that learning is a necessary action, that it is *doing something* more than just waiting and honing my physical form, I dressed in a fresh tactical jumpsuit, loaded up my touch-tablet, laced up my boots, pulled my long, wavy, and greasily-in-need-of-washing brown hair back into a tight bun, and decided to encourage the treat of some early endorphins by running all the way to the City Safety offices on Ponce de Leon.

Down the lift and out onto the streets the day was humming with a subtle tension. Maybe it was just an anxiety inside of me stirred with thoughts of a killer, a Sacred killer, or maybe it was real and generalizable, a tension in the crowds I ran around or through—we have surveys and studies that have shown a greater frequency of *the Dream*, and other traumatic expressions in the build-up to *The Great Day of Mourning*.

I ran under the I-20 park overpass and north on Moreland for a couple of miles, and then veered north and west into Inman Park, a neighborhood with its own flavor of diverse pantheon clustering and displays, and a good place to adjoin my run to others who enjoy an ancient footpath or Greenway that has been retain and further developed for our times and technologies.

Between the buildings and pylons, and below the observational decks and patios for relaxation and breakfast and socializing, I ran with a group of other runners forming and reforming around me. I felt wild and natural and truly human, and not unlike I understood how fish once moved in a school or wolves in a pack. Panting and breathing together, the plant rubber of my boots—all the boots and shoes—beating the road, the endorphins released and spread through me, and I felt everything and then nothing in the best way. I felt the pack around me and through me and we breathed with one breath. In. And one breath. Out.

I let go. And we ran.

Approaching the massively wide, old brick building that is the base structure of City Safety, I regained myself and peeled off from the group saying nothing. The temporal change into the building helped cool the sweat from my brow and I quickly visited the sanitation room for a towel to further cool and comfort my body. I zipped down my jumpsuit and wiped where I needed before zipping up and entering my shared work pod. I extended greetings on the way, but most of my co-workers were either not in yet, or had no plans to be in today, as preparations for tomorrow loomed large for most of us.

There it was on my desk, the volume of Filipino mythos, tales from that long-gone island nation, that live still in our Archives and the hearts and minds of various practitioners and adherents around this Domed-world.

I turned to the stories of Dayang Masalanta that I book-marked yesterday after I perused. Now I had time for thoroughness. Now was the fulfillment and application of work.

She was connected to her mountain, a protector and in some ways an avatar for that bold landmass, Mount Makiling, a bent or leaning structure, as its Tagalog name implies; one seen from some angles as a reclining woman. She was by origin a *diwata* or *anitu*, maybe an ancestor spirit turned natural woodland being.

Most of the tales described her as a woman collecting lovers, as men disappear on or about the mountain. In others, she is the spurned lover and disappearances are her revenge. In still more, she helps lost lovers connect with their true partners. Congruent with what we know about the world before the Katastrophe, her kindness was often met with greed. She could turn ginger into gold, and to people then, that soft, malleable metal was given ridiculous and dangerous value beyond its own material merits.

I read it all, every variation, every interpretation. My work extended into other volumes from our library. The woman I had met yesterday on that mountain, who captivated me like the deity she sought to embody captivated the peoples around Mount Makiling and Laguna, Philippines, had trained and studied deeply. I had read everything my world knew by way of recorded history about this figure, and she clearly knew this figure on a deeper level. Her understanding was personal and practiced.

The leap between what I had now read and what she lived was the divide of faith and commitment. It was that leap, and the dark mystery of that divide, that excited all the parts of me and how I experienced this new work of mine at Sacred Safety and living here in this City.

The Next Bardo

Rings within rings within rings within rings. From an outer ring down to the white face of a demon with red eyes and a red tongue at an angry dangle. Blue waves, contoured flourishes, greens of hills, and Devanāgarī script. A world at each inner level. And a level of consciousness dropping and deepening. From the edges to the center. And the demon awaits.

The mandala hung on the wall of the family's dining room, the image at the center of a wide, silk tapestry, red with a saffron trim. It drew my attention as my hunger mounted and the vast aromas, sounds, and actions of preparation filled the rest of my senses.

I had spent the day at the Sacred Safety office, even lunching at my desk, before my legs needed to move and

I instinctively knew the daytime was coming to a close.

Promptly at 6:01pm my wristwatch buzzed, and I touched-up my tablet to receive a message from Thinkowitz.

By that point I was on a tram passing Midtown into Buckhead, moving north towards where he lived. He seemed to have deduced my trajectory, because he suggested I meet him to go speak to Pearl Iko's family. I got off the tram at the Sandy Springs platform where I last saw him yesterday, and there he was to greet me.

We took a tram on a higher platform north-northeast toward Duluth. The central Duluth tram stop was within the building where Pearl Iko's family lived. It was a wide apartment that took up the whole floor and contained multiple related family units. I had visited other such large, connected family dwellings in the suburbs. Where and how my parents lived in Roswell was much smaller and private. And lower, but the view here off the tram, out over Duluth, the square down below, a wide-limbed climbing tree for children and splash pad was delightful.

"Tashi delek," said the small, old woman who greeted us at the door.

"Tashi delek shu," replied my partner while he put his hands together and nodded at the same time as the woman.

She led us inside and told us her name was Dawa Dongtotsang. Her husband was named Nima, and I clasped hands with them both. They were the parents of Pearl Iko. They were both slightly taller than me, maybe five six, five seven, but seemed sunken, and understandably so. Their skin was like turmeric and their dark hair was thick and wavy. It was clearly dinner time and there was a lot of activity going on around the home. But it was hushed and solemn as the news Lisa-Marie Sicily delivered earlier in the day had clearly made its way through the family.

Thinkowitz and I were seated on a rug with a pattern not too dissimilar from the mandala tapestry on the wall. The rug was wide and filled most of the main room, and it was hard to take in the whole pattern. Across the empty center of the rug before us were two people about the same ages as Dawa and Nima. We were introduced to Pearl Iko's aunt and uncle, Norlha and Choegyal Dongtotsang.

Everyone in the family was wearing saffron jump suits of satin that zippered up, and similar in design to mine of dark blue cotton. No touch panels or fabrics. Just saffron, shimmering in its satin ripples, with a crimson trim all around.

It was while sitting on the rug, just before the food was served that I was captivated by the hanging mandala, drawing me out of the room and the work and the interactions, and sending me back deep into myself where I had mostly hidden all day.

Extended family sat further out from this center ring as the food was served on the rug, and I struggled to keep up with all of the names, but all were said, and every face acknowledge by me and my partner. As soon as all the brass and copper platters of provisions were brought into the center, they were immediately circulated around the perimeter by active hands and empty plates arrived in front of me and Thinkowitz before the first offering came by.

With my hand—just like the young woman to my right and to Thinkowitz's left—I took a little of every cuisine that passed on a platter before me. The woman to my right was named Tendon Dongtotsang, and the woman to Thinkowitz's left was named Dolma Dongtotsang. Someone called them "the twins," and someone chuckled, but they looked nothing alike.

My plate was a feast of color and flavor and aromas. Rice, buckwheat, potatoes, turnips, beans. As I broke open a small spongy cake, and the sharp spice scent filled my nostrils, Tendon guided me.

"That is tsampa," she said. "Here, try this hot sauce on it."

I did, and it opened up my sinuses to such a degree that I felt my eyebrows tingle. From the back of the room a deep and frightening hum began. It rooted and rumbled in the base of my spine, and I turned around to see eight shaven-headed men and women in the same saffron jumpsuits as everyone else seated in the lotus position and chanting. I could feel the sound in each bite. A bell sounded, more a ting than a ring.

I overheard Dolman naming for Thinkowitz the next thing on my plate that I didn't recognize. She called it *momo*. Such a strange coincidence, but not uncommon in the convergence of language and culture that filled the quotidian of our world.

I made the first bite of the momo on my plate. It was a chewy dumpling, its casing mushing and tearing with my teeth, and then I cut into juicy shreds of cabbage tingling my lips and tongue with ginger and garlic.

It was a level of sensuality and the pleasures of presence in the body that reminded me of what I understood about mystical, devotional, and even avatarian experiences.

We were here to respectively grieve with the family, but also ask some questions. The questions were important for our investigation, for the greater good of our whole world and all citizens, but their grief needed to be respected too. It was hard to rest my mind, to focus on the food, to feel the chanting, the tingle up my spine with each bell, each hard, clear ting. And the mandala to me from the wall. I wanted to actively work on the case, the cases. But I wasn't alone here. And it wasn't only about me.

Our questions went to the "twins," Dolma and Tendon. It turned out they were not twins at all, but double cousins. Their fathers were brothers and married to sisters. The weddings happened in the same month. The conceptions happened in the same following month. And the girls were born in the same month later that year. Pearl Iko was Dolma's younger sister.

We asked if Pearl ever spent time at New Gibraltar. We asked if she, as far as they knew, knew someone named Dayang Masalanta. As this was all quickly determined to the negative, I started to wonder what we were doing here. Her death seemed random, and impulsive, not personal.

Tendon was also double cousins with Pearl Iko, as she was with Dolma. She explained that this ritual in the moment felt like a homecoming for Pearl although she has never really been gone. A couple of years ago she started to spend time with a young man who worshipped Tsukuyomi, the Japanese god of the moon. As they fell in love, she really appreciated how his moon deity was masculine. She accordingly appreciated that the sun deity was feminine.

Pearl let go of her birthname, Choden Dongtotsang, and embraced a new name that felt closer for her to the language and culture of her goddess, Ama-terasu, and the Shinto faith around the goddess. The love for the young man faded, but not for the goddess. Her path progressed all the way to avatarism.

It felt like there was no more use for questioning. I felt the depth of the grief in the slow deliberate appreciation for food around me, and the guttural hum of the throat-singing filled the space. I returned to the tsampa and momo, the warmth and the spices. A ting from a bell seemed to hang in the air forever.

The Master First and Last

Full, sated and somber, we rode a high, express tram due north to where the Dome meets the Earth.

"It's not where I expected it to be," I finally spoke.

"What did you expect? Around the base of the Dome is where all control and maintenance facilities sit."

"It's silly. I guess I always expected it would be at the top of a tower or pylon deep in the City, either near City Safety on Ponce or City Hall on Trinity. Like an aviary of flags, feathers, streamers, and windvanes testing the most potent edge of our air that has risen beyond the strain of our world," I confessed.

"That is a very romantic and mythic conceptualization, Casaubon. I have always been confident that you have the sensitivity for our work. But what matters most for our technologies is functionality, not thematic styling.

"We fashion the tools to save ourselves. In my tradition, we thank Hashem for creating us with such love. Our Psalm 139 states, '*I praise you, for I am fearfully and wonderfully made.*' But alas, this is in your tradition too. I believe most of us interpret our respective, personal theologies to incorporate such concepts. In our Profane world of copious Sanctities, we take responsibility for our own human failings. We all helped kill the dead god with a capital 'K', but he took many—nay, most—with him. Our victory is somber like our hope.

"In our new world we look ourselves and our technologies in the eyes, so to speak. The dog will wag the tail. Don't you remember the Dome-Emergency-Maintenance training we all got in our early schooling. Even those who engage in a deification of our technologies accept that those gods of theirs are in service to the Greater Good in those functions."

I had a slight, reflexive shudder to the words *Greater Good*, but I tried to ignore it.

"In this Domed-world," he continued. "We understand that survival doesn't mean simply breathing, having a beating heart, not being dead. To survive as a people, a humanity, a society, we must fully live, in the totality of human expression. Kapital is dead, and with *him*…"

He sort of snarled the word, *him*. And paused. I'd never really heard him like this. The cases must be getting to him. We spoke intimately, sitting side-by-side, but we were public and other passengers around us seemed to be listening. His voice had this quality, an ease and authority, an ease with authority, and it drew in others.

" …What died with *him* is the punishing compulsion to work. It is almost as abhorrent to us as greed. Our current compulsion is to serve. It is a compulsion of self-preservation to dampen the fire of guilt that burns in us.

"Just look at Lamon Phonsavanh, who you met yesterday, for example. His chosen work involves gentleness. He operates a gallery in Midtown that features exhibits of gentleness for the audience to interact with. Soap bubbles, Casaubon. A whole room of soap bubbles. No touch surfaces, just soap bubbles popping in from all four corners. Sometimes I go there to sit and meditate. Sometimes I bring my children to his exhibit of cotton balls. A room of soft puffs of various colors. We swim through the softness and enjoy an experience that can only be had through gentleness. His current effort, an effort that he has committed his life to, is for the benefit of us all, for the Greater Good. We need gentleness. For him, as for us in our efforts, it is not *work*, in the sense that Kapital used to crush us with.

"Remember one of the key texts from your youthful education, Profane Prophet Paul Lafargue's *The Right to Be Lazy*. Lafargue reminds us of Antipater who wrote of the advent of the waterwheel, and how it would help his world. He wrote, '*Cease from grinding, ye women who toil at the mill... Demeter has ordered the Nymphs to perform the work of your hands, and they leaping down on top of the wheel, turn its axle.*' See how he playfully interprets the science through deification, and is socially excited that the women slaves will be freed from their work. The citizens of his world will 'feast on the products of Demeter without labor' as we do here today for each of our respective gods.

"We were not ready yet. We did not understand freedom nor community fully. But now, sadly—or gladly, Casaubon—we have been humbled. Now we live the dream—in our humbled, somber way, free of ego and gloating—of the Greek poet Antipater, of the ancients who enjoyed luxury, philosophy, and arts, and yet understood that life only really existed for them through the practice of slavery. And that practice continued either by wage or whip until the birth and then ubiquity of Kapital. That dream, in the poetry of Antipater, hinges upon technology because that is what we humans have always done. We fashion tools to make easier our endeavors.

"The Dome is our water wheel. But it is so much more. The Dome is our righteous Babel, and the Heavens that we have reached is the one we have created here on

Earth. Our Resurga. As you know, we took that word from Dante, from the great mountain like a tower that he built, his Purgatorio. We all learn the line as children— *Ma qui la morta poesì resurga, o sante Muse, poi che vostro sono*—Rise again from the dead, my poetry, oh holy Muse, for I am yours.

"In that epic poem, as the dead rose through the levels of the mountain, they shed their guilt and their sin, rising and purifying. Thus us in the raising of the Dome. We have purified and healed this patch of Earth under the Dome. We are healing the people, the community under the Dome. The Dome is our poetry and we each have our own Muse, our own abstraction of focus, worship, veneration, submission, empowerment. Our mountain is everything to us, our Purgatorio, our Greylock."

"What is Greylock?" I asked.

"Yesterday, we stood on New Gibraltar, and I mentioned that there was a Profane association with a similar place. One of our great Profane Scriptures was inspired by a mountain."

A small crowd had formed around us in seats and with some people standing, leaning in. Thinkowitz didn't seem to notice, or at least he didn't change the way he spoke. I was the student he was focusing on, but his address was loud enough for all to hear.

I tightened my brow. Actively following my senior

partner and mentor, I was making mental notes of all he said, and worked to contextualize all the information he shared with me into real knowledge. He had already mentioned *Purgatorio*, but we don't generally think of that book as Profane. It is a Sacred text that can transmit wisdom beyond the theological limits of a faith into a more universal or secular perspective. As often happens, I didn't know where his words would lead, but I trusted that that is where learning happened.

"You are familiar with *Moby-Dick* and what that text has to teach us about democracy and empathy and the fundamental connectiveness of humanity," he continued. "At the center of the story is the titular white whale, of course.

"For Herman Melville that whiteness was terrifying. It represented a complete and total emptiness, an absence, a lack. To esteem whiteness seemed like a betrayal of the truth of humanity and the universe for Melville. Darkness is worth exploring, darkness hints at mystery, things unseen, things to be uncovered and revealed. White says no, there is nothing. This is all there is. White is hopeless.

"In the novel, his hero Ishmael takes this critique to the metaphysical and declares: *Though in many of its aspect this visible world seems formed in love, the invisible spheres were formed in fright*."

A motley array of people all around us, some now sitting

on the floor of the tram at our feet, nodded and exhaled *ahs* and *aws*. I read the faces peripherally and kept my attention to my mentor.

"Melville originally envision a black whale. He wrote at a desk before a window and out that window was Mount Greylock, the tallest mountain in the state of Massachusetts. As winter set in and snow fell, the mountain was soon covered. From his view, the contours of the mountain looked like humps, and now snow-covered they looked like the head and hump of a white whale, the whole mountain a color-less sperm whale and inspiration for the great cetacean beast of the deep, Moby Dick. In the mountain he found his subject, not just the whale, but its whiteness.

"What he understood about that frightful whiteness, gazing there those long hours into its pronounced and profound absence was that into this void we can project and then find anything. But a tabula rasa is never pure. Terror corrupts, anxiety influences. Freedom, and the power it holds, is also terrifying and anxiety-inducing," said Thinkowitz.

As he said this, I pictured not the rock mountain, but the total touch-box clean, white room of the first session stage at Mystical Embrace. In that space the deepest desire for deification connection—a that-which-fundamentally-makes-us-human connection—, a desire born out of love, which is projected back to us from the blankness, can also be one of terror.

—

"Clearly, we humans have difficulty with our ability to rest in mystery. For four hundred years before the Katastrophe we let Kapital frightfully and tragically fill our need for Abstraction. But we are now—sadly, or gladly—ever-crippled to fill the greatest of abstractions in a more sympathetic way.

"For Melville, Greylock was a magic mountain which taught, or reminded, or clarified all of this for him. It is hard for some of us to contextualize the Dome from above or outside. New Gibraltar, the smooth, white mountainous rock is an appropriate analog of the Dome. Our Greylock, an empty signifier, once was a monument in praise of the evil of humanity, the awfulness people can do to people whom they choose to other, two hundred years ago; alien concepts to us now, and sand-blast-cleansed in its own time.

"Just look at it, Casaubon. Think of yesterday, the multitude atop, and in such displays. Our beautiful plurality. New Gibraltar, like the Dome, is our White Whale.

"And of all the wonders and Profane prophecies within that scripture, the whole context for that story, whaling, destroying these magisterial animals, was an industry that was winding down toward the fated day that we mourn tomorrow. August 28, 1859 was the day oil was first drilled in the state of Pennsylvania. That day began the Kapitalist project through which we destroyed the

Earth and our civilizations. That is the day that ushered in the Katastrophe, that found the energy source to power the death-drive in the green-eyed god, Kapital, and it is that global climate Katastrophe that took so many of us away with the Earth. Kapital fell, and we bear the wound of its excision," said Sacred Detective Rabbinowitz, and paused for a moment as if to make sure we were all with him, if not just me.

"We continue to heal today, every day a little more, and this wound is turning to scar tissue, metaphorically. We have been humbled, and through that humbling we rise up together like we raised our Dome. And as the Dome harnesses the power of the Sun, we have the freedom to work if and when we choose, and the freedom for repose and to chill when we choose. We have a shared objective and goal together with and within the Dome. The Dome establishes and upholds our new reality. Outside the Dome, the Sun is a death-star. Inside, it is our infinite reactor, source of life, and household battery.

"Remember, Casaubon," he said, while granting a smile and general nod to the throng around us. "I am myself an example of the success of our Domed-world. The SunSpot Cyborg Program took me on as one of its first test subjects. This was as much due to my dire situation as to what has been described as my willful tenacity. I pushed my body beyond its physical limitations, but my mind was inhospitable and opaque to me. I experienced the world through a limited frame.

"But harnessing the power of the Sun, an ancient dream clearly expressed by Profane Prophet Nikolai Tesla, a man who was motivated by the belief that we are all one in spite of the contemporaneous terror of Kapital, allowed all of our technological dreams to flow forth. The process of the Program augmented and maximized the natural power of my brain, healing and then enhancing what I had suffered since birth.

"As Lafargue wrote in 1883, *Aristotle's dream is our reality*. And I am proof of this. *Our machines breath fire, have limbs of steel, never grow weary, never need to sleep. They are marvelously productive and behave docilely—even as they go about their sacred work. The machine is humanity's savior*. He called the machine 'the god who will redeem man and give him leisure and liberty.'

"This is all part of our re-enchantment. Our re-enchantment is enacted upon several levels, Casaubon. We are as enchanted now about our technologies as we are with personalized deification, with the fulfillment we can feel with creativity, sanctity, and connection with something beyond ourselves. I connect with a tradition as well as a god, a theology, and a body of laws. Others in the City are finding connection with gods and the experience of learning about those gods. They are doing research in the same way I am pursuing tradition through a hermeneutic.

"We live in a secular society which respects human

—
82

freedom. Henotheism and agnosticism are our great accepting. The greatest human freedom is in what to believe even if ultimately it is in nothing. Faith is Somber-Hope," he said, bringing us back to such familiar refrains for how our world holds itself together that it felt to all of us like closure.

My partner has at times mentioned his *daf yomi* to me, the daily page of Talmud that he reads. Sometimes our interactions felt like he was providing a page for me from his own text of experience and understanding. This moment on the tram, for me, and likely the devoted crowd of fellow humans around us—many of whom had clearly travelled beyond their destination just to keep listening—was a perfect encapsulation of why he is sometimes referred to by the same name as the author of Ecclesiastes, Qoheleth. It is an ancient Hebrew word that can be translated as teacher, but also as "the encyclopedic mind."

As we approached the Cumming tram stop, it was as if the sky of our whole world bent towards our inevitable horizon, and a view once vast was made an illusion by its undeniable limit.

Don't Hold Your Breath (or Divine Symmetry)

It was a short walk from the tram pylon's base, and then before us, tucked in the bottom curve of the Dome meeting the earth, sat a small, gray, concrete building, functional, and unassuming.

We were greeted at the door by the operator on duty. Sacred Detective Rabbinowitz sent word of our visit and confirmed who was attending this evening.

"Evening greetings! I'm Sāgo Butterworm! Welcome to the BDMS! I'm excited to tour you and show you the facilities here, but, well, I'm sad about why you are here, though."

The sadness was shown, but not for long. They was giddy and playful. Which was not what I expected from someone in such a moribund-seeming profession. It was late in the evening, early night. Maybe they doesn't get a lot of visitors?

We followed them into the facility. I observed their height at being just under my partner's, so about six feet and maybe an inch. They had straight, dark, hair, tight on the sides and the top a shiny swoop, bumped out and curved back. Their skin was creamy like my own, but a little darker, like the milk we make from oats. Taupe linen pants and a white sleeveless t-shirt were all they wore over a lithe frame, and a bracelet of red thread-strung red beads—reminiscent of so many beads at the Dongtotsang home—was the only accent to their outfit.

The whole facility was one simple room. The far wall that abutted the Dome was lined with a long desk and a touch wall, touched-up to a screen showing a glowing thermal map of our Domed-world. Life teemed in darker concentration in the City proper, and flowed out in oranges and yellows—some saffron like a theme of the evening—with clusters of red into the suburbs. Three chairs sat at the desk before the touch wall. To the right was a door to a bathroom, the only break in the rectangle of the room. The left wall was lined by a kitchen counter of machinery for culinary needs and three stools. The center of the room was wide open and, in its center, lay a cerulean rug with one pink circle of a pillow at its center. Extra pillows were stacked in the corner to the left of the door.

When Sāgo Butterworm closed the door behind us, the most compelling thing about the space was its total absence of sound. It was a silence you felt. The touched-up screen on the wall glowed and pulsed in the different thermal colors of life, and numbers ticked up and down in small modulations charting the breath components of our controlled air. But in total silence.

"We do not get visitors often here, so this is a real treat! Oh, and also, I've read all about you, Sacred Detective Rabbinowitz. And your partner too, hello to you!" They led us around the room, barefoot, but still avoiding walking on the rug, and we followed respectively.

"I love what you do, but so sad the reasons you have to do it, people dying and being hurt and stuff. But I love the connections and sorting through all the mythologies and deities. Oh my OM, there are so many gods and goddesses! So many! And believe me, I've tried a few."

"Thank you, Sāgo. And yes, you are correct. It can be very difficult and very fulfilling at the same time. We've tried to make our world simple because humans can be so complicated. I've visited this facility before, last year the last time, but before you came on, I believe?" Thinkowitz asked as an invitation. He knew the answer.

"Yes! I am the new one. The newbie. The new third. The newt. I only started in May, but there are always three operators working in rotation. We are like the Fates! The Moirai! But actually, it's so cool. Imberline Jane worships one of the Moirai. She has been here the longest too. It's so holistic, her work and her worship. It's all one! But she's so great. She has taught me so much."

The speed and energy by which he talked and moved—a performance of physical punctuation of points and words —was the aural accompaniment to the constant movement of colors and numbers on the screen wall.

"She has been like my mentor here. Imberline Jane worships Clotho, the first of the Moirai. She who spins. I love her so much! And Chen Hui too! Oh my OM! She has also been such a help. Like a big sister! Chen Hui worships the Chinese goddess Feng Po Po, the goddess of winds, and storms, and moisture. So holistic! I'm always in awe."

After the minimal tour around the rug and obvious space, they led us to the stools at the kitchen wall and we sat at their direction while they continued to stand and iterate with hands and movements from almost every joint in their body.

"Casaubon, I brought you here to see the facility and have an understanding of the actual citizens, the humans, who monitor the technology of the Breath/Death

Monitoring System. Meeting Sāgo Butterworm is a wonderful bonus for us, even on the sad occasion of our work," said my partner in lead.

"So the machine, the System, monitors air-content for human and animal breath working alongside the main controls and filtration of our ambient air inside of the Dome. What do you and the other operators do here on your shifts, Sāgo?" I assessed and asked.

"I wait, I contemplate! I practice yoga, and I meditate!" Each phrasing had an accompanying movement. Each moment of rhyme punctuated with gesture.

"We keep hand-written accounts of all activity," they continued at their most calm and professional. "While a computer monitoring breath tells us about the levels, even as precise as they are, it is us who make sense out of that data. We human operators understand the technology and make a determination of what it means. The machine documents breath, we document death." They pointed over at the notebooks on the desk before the screen wall. "That part is very sad, but thankfully it doesn't happen every shift."

"You have emphasized how holistic the work and worship of your co-operator is. Who do you worship, Sāgo?" I asked.

"Oh my OM, that is funny! And I am so proud of myself that I have talked all about these wonderful women who have welcomed me into this new job and not just myself. It is also funny too, because I am trying to be so holistic that it feels like I am expressing—do you like that, *expressing*—my devotion in every breath I take in or let out. I took this position as an operator at the BDMS as a path in a holistic life."

They hopped up onto a sitting position on the kitchen counter and seemed to calm into their story.

"So, I was a mess. Worshipping a different deity each week it felt like. Romantic and sexual partners were easier to match with than all of these deities. There were years of this, and the more random and esoteric the better. Living more for others and trying to impress my friends.

That is what it felt like. I have a lot of really cool, creative friends. So, it is understandable, but I was neglecting myself. That was all until I met Kiki Selavy," they said.

"The Hecate-worshipper, who does the big moonlight, roof-top yoga events? We met her at a moon deity event at the Fox back in January," I said, feeling like Thinkowitz, watching my own mind connect and advert in our work.

"Oh yes, Oh OM, that is she! She saved me. I didn't realize that I needed some mothering, mine didn't make it..." they paused briefly, sullenly, like hitting an emotional bump in their progress, until their energy level

89

surged back up. "I went to one full moon yoga session back in February, since some of my friends were going, and so I went, and it felt so good! I was so awful at the asanas back then. Ha! After, I asked her for some additional instruction. And Kiki, she saved me, and introduced me to the mother of all sounds. So, I have a new mother, and she has me, with every breath I take. And give back."

"Yes?" I was puzzled.

"Sāgo Butterworm worships Om, the mother of all sounds, which dates back to the earliest Vedic texts and continues as a concept into most progressions off of that tradition," my partner clarified to me.

"Oh my OM, yes! I'm so sorry, Detective. I worship Om! Yes, Om! It might be the mother of all sounds, but I see breath as genderless and a deity of my own understanding. I had explored life through the different genders, and uhg, so many different gods and goddesses, and none of it felt right. Now like breath, I have no gender, and I worship that animating force, the life-sustaining *spiritus* that flows through us all!

"So, your work here is devotional, and that is part of your commitment?" I asked.

"Yes! This is like a sad and Sacred duty. And it brings me peace. I have given myself, and I continue to give every breath, to helping everyone in our world in this work. I wait, I contemplate. I practice yoga, and I meditate! Breath is about balance. The work of the BDMS, of myself and Imberline Jane and Chen Hui helps keep balance in our world. I believe it is similar to what you Sacred Detectives do, too."

I rose from the stool with my partner who thanked Sāgo Butterworm for that sentiment, and I concurred.

"And as far as you can tell, with the diagnostics you ran between my call and our arrival, everything with the BDMS is operational and in-line?" Thinkowitz asked the facility operations monitor.

"Yes! Only one new death since yesterday and recorded earlier in the hand of Chen Hui who was on shift before my arrival."

"Do you have any further questions, Casaubon?" my partner asked.

When I said no, and offered a goodbye to our host, Thinkowitz told me he had decided to stay longer, to meditate with Sāgo and learn more about breath.

I took no offense to being excluded and watched Sāgo bring another pillow to the cerulean rug. Thinkowitz removed his coat, hanging it on a chair, as well as his hat, a kippah still present beneath, before sitting on the squat pink pillow.

I said another goodbye to both of them as Sāgo sat on their pillow. As I was passing through the door out into the night, I heard Sāgo speak:

"Oh my OM! Did you know that the word *animal* come from *animare* in Latin which means *to fill with breath* like that is what we are as animals, breath-filled things?"

I was sure Sacred Detective Rabbi Jakob Rabbinowitz, nicknamed "Thinkowitz" by cruel children in his youth before his cyborg enhancements, a name he now bears as an ironic triumph, did already know that, but wasn't going to let on since he was here to listen and learn.

Wild is the Wind

My tram car was empty. This was a rare moment on a tram into the City from the suburbs, and I took advantage of it. All of the citizens who rode well past their destinations to this final stop while listening to the pontifications of my partner were long gone.

I drew out my touch-tablet from its pocket in my jumpsuit and searched the Archive for the music of Nina Simone. I started the first song that caught my eye.

"I Want a Little Sugar in My Bowl" filled the car. That voice—so alive and warm and rich and oaken—filled me too, and I felt something coo and purr in the center of me and expand out in wavey lines to the ends of my nerves.

I wanted to take this feeling home to bed with me. But it

was only a moment on the tram. With a song. This case, or these cases, won't allow me any real respite or pleasure. Or I won't allow myself. Every death in our world feels personal, every loss of breath is a ripple through all of us in the Dome. But most grievous, most paining, is when the death is violent, when it is intentional. The peace of our world was earned and inherited in the worst way possible.

Horns and a piano blasted and banged a rhythm with rests between loud pronouncements in the next song. The moving air of the tram car was alive just for me. I was tired, but my blood rose to the beat. The purr at my center was revving up. I wasn't *feeling good* necessarily, but I was feeling a sense of purpose that softened anxiety. Her voice and those words empowered me and gave me the sense that we can do this, we can find and stop this killer, that we can find Aho'eitu.

Stars when you shine, you know how I feel...

Between towers and pylons under this dome, stars refracting through our fishbowl, the tram headed south taking me home to the City.

The Damage Today

The call came blasting through a squishy sea of sleep, ringing out at emergency levels and drawing my mind up from restful depths. Then I was up, suited, and out to the location point that my partner had sent with all of my readiness and training activated.

I approached Sacred Detective Rabbinowitz at the northwest corner of Peachtree Street—running north to south—and Peachtree Place running east to west. We were only five large blocks south of The Temple of Delphi and Tartarus below, on 15th Street. That is where we were called on my first case with Sacred Safety and Thinkowitz after I transferred from Profane. The Temple of Delphi was in an old, large wood building from the early 20th century with a stone foundation. That is where Tiresias Pythia gave prophecy. The office below the

Temple in the same building is where Tartarus sat, a funereal pit, impossibly deep, a dark hole of pure blackness, a place and a god for veneration, operated by N'Deye Frimbo. We solved the murder of Tiresias Pythia, and I had the opportunity of meeting Frimbo and beholding the frightful might of Tartarus.

I found my partner standing and staring down at my newest threshold level of horror and violence.

What I was seeing didn't make much sense at my first glance, nor as I tried to focus. A perimeter was established around the scene and four Profane Safety officers blocked for us a viewing area from passers-by and the concerned crowd that ebbed in and out to see if we needed assistance. Some people passed in tears and wished us the best, many giving blessings and prayers from their various gods.

Hector Prudhomme, a Profane Safety Officer who worshipped Phoebus Apollo, took photographs of everything before us. I recognized him from various cases I worked when I was in Profane, and I gave him a brief nod. Then it was right back to trying to understand what I was looking at.

It was a tangle and a pile, blood-soaked and broken. The heap of body parts and fabric looked sudden and unintentional. I saw three feminine arms, two of darker skin than the third, one thin smooth dark leg with no shoe on its long foot with pink toe nail polish draped over a white touch blanket dripping blood that one arm emerged from along with silky, straight black hair and beneath that, the source for three of the limbs and a crown of kinky black hair.

Sacred Detective Rabbinowitz was silently studying the bulky mass and the sidewalk all around it. My partner, without moving his head from its vantage point, asked to no one in particular, "what do we know?"

Hector Prudhomme replied: "The witness—Blanche Greene, a woman who was getting her breakfast café ready to open—who notified City Safety, saw a man, not striking in size or touch-up features, struggling to carry the blanket over one shoulder and a bloody Assata Yemi over the other shoulder. The light was still hazy, and the towers cut shadows across the ground in obstructive patterns. When she caught a glimpse of Yemi's face in that brief moment of seeing this man repositioning the body on his shoulder, she screamed and drew attention to him. He dropped both items and ran off up one block to Tenth Street and then right towards Piedmont Park. A few people who helped out in her café chased after him, but lost him in the Park. I've sent four officers to search the Park." He then returned to photography.

When Hector seemed satisfied with the amount of photographs he had taken, he paused and looked at my partner who then gave an affirmative nod.

Hector put his camera away and motioned for two other

officers to join him and they carefully lifted the soggy, red and white blanket mass and laid it next to the body beneath. Before they unwrapped the blanket, there was a scream. Someone passing had seen what lay beneath and then we all did.

The poor woman. Her face had been beaten in, concave, crushed, unrecognizable. Her hair was in a large round Afro, and blood had dried into it. She wore a long simple cotton dress in a blue and white tie-dyed pattern. Several beaded necklaces bunched across her neck and breast. The only other wounds besides her face appeared separate, most likely from being dropped. There was a white ballet slipper on her left foot.

"All I can say about the result of the force that was necessary to make a wound of this size and depth is that she would have suffered for a brief moment. It would have been immense, but brief," said Sacred Detective Rabbinowitz before adding, "There is something very familiar about her," and then, "*Baruch Hashem.*"

Hector Prudhomme drew his camera and took a few photographs and then nodded for two of the other officers to unwrap the blanket. As I suspected, we now found Pearl Iko. Five feet and two inches, a skintight touch suit, and the face that I had seen in the gold frame at the Dongtotsang home. Her throat was missing. I heard another, "*Baruch Hashem,*" behind me.

As Hector returned to photography, my partner backed

up slowly and looking down at his feet, pivoted one hundred and eighty degrees and kept on south on the Peachtree Street sidewalk. The ground tram rode by going north up Peachtree Street, and I looked back at the two women laying side-by-side, Pearl Iko on the blanket, the other woman on the sidewalk, one shoe, necklaces, and rings on her fingers.

Thinkowitz was following a blood trail, faint, sporadic, and well-stepped on, but south on the sidewalk. It led across 8th Street and to a large splatter of blood and what looked like a tooth or teeth in the shadowed corner of a building. A white ballet shoe and a knitted-yarn sack striped in red, black, green, and yellow were adjacent to the puddle.

Another officer and Hector followed and stood by attentively waiting to document with photography and notes. Thinkowitz loosened the drawstring and opened the bag. Sewn just within the opening was a cloth note on which was printed: *if found please return to Assata Yemi 418 Midtown Towers 7th and Cypress*.

"So, her name is Assata Yemi, and she lives just around the corner from here?" I stated the obvious new details as if in a question, as I was still trying to read the situation.

"Witnesses on the block between 8th Street and Peachtree Place noted that the victim, who is not Pearl Iko, the other victim, has passed this way—south on the sidewalk of Peachtree Street—at the same time of morning, just after dawn, almost every day for the last few months," added Hector who had spoken to all of the officers who canvased the area.

"Can you read the details present and understand what happened here?" I asked my partner.

Hector and the other officer went to work around this second crime scene to document, preserve, and understand.

"What I read here, Assistant Sacred Detective Edwina Casaubon, is a narrative that you can help assemble with me," began my partner. "It appears that this is where the violence took place, at this corner. That the perpetrator was carrying Pearl Iko wrapped in the blanket and then encountered Assata Yemi here, most likely suddenly. She was then struck in the face with enormous force, and then lifted up on his shoulder and carried north on the sidewalk of Peachtree Street."

"So, she was heading home, and he was taking her back where she came from after he did this?" I reasoned.

"That is what appears in the details," he said.

"Do you think they knew each other? Look how he brutalized her face, like he tried to make her unrecognizable. Trying to erase her face."

"We cannot assume the why, but that interpretation does seem possible in the narrow target of the violence," said Thinkowitz.

"She walks this way almost every day at this time, heading home from somewhere, we can assume, since her home is around the block that way from here. Pearl Iko was killed or at least removed from Mystical Embrace south and west of here. Maybe the perpetrator was bringing her north and runs into Assata Yemi and immediately kills her and then tries to continue north and bring her with him? And still no sign of 'Aho'eitu?" I assessed.

"Yes, Casaubon, your training from Profane Safety in reading the details of human interactions is just as applicable here in Sacred. There is more to know, and the most occult aspect of our work, *the why*, lies as the greatest mystery."

Sacred Detective Rabbinowitz paced around the sidewalk corner. He looked up Peachtree Street. And then down the street.

"We assume he was taking them both that way, but we do not know where. However, Casaubon, we do have a guess as to where she was going…"

Satisfy This Hungriness

Midtown Towers was one of four buildings that made up the block between 7th and 8th Streets to the south and north on West Peachtree and Cypress Street to the west and east. The foundations of all four buildings were from the late 21st century and after the tenth floor the rest is all Post-Katastrophe titanium and carbon clean, dark design. The original levels had been updated while still retaining that late 21st century ironic and despairing aesthetic of a period when the first mass island and dessert deaths were happening. The human is a strange creator. It is understandable the Somber-Hope we express within this thriving Dome.

We took the lift to the fourth floor and found her door.

We knocked on the neighbor's door at 417, bird noises like a shrill and repetitive *pee-wit* sounded from within. A woman with a wide white and rippling body in a wide and rippling white robe, long silver hair pulled down the left side of her neck and incorporated into the folds of her robe answered. She was lovely and reminded me of a paler version of my mother.

"Pardon us, but we are with City Safety—I'm Sacred Detective Jakob Rabbinowitz and this is my partner, Assistant Detective Edwina Casaubon—and what might be a literal *tragedy* seems to have befallen your neighbor Assata Yemi. May I ask your name?" said my partner, and giving me a bit of a shock that he would already assess this to be a Sacred crime and tragic. But I guess it did seem to be related to what happened to Pearl Iko.

"Oh dear, thank you for telling me, Detectives. My name is Delta Marsh. I was just finishing my morning ablutions. I worship Tiddy Mun, a bog deity from England, and I would love to tell you both all about him, but it seems you are on such sad and serious business. And I'm so sorry. Assata was such a dear."

"Did you know her well?" I asked.

"Well, dear, I wish I did. She was very nice but had only moved in a couple of months ago. April first exactly. And she was very nice to chat with when we ran into each other, but she mostly kept to herself. She was very devout, and seemed to be on a new path, a very healing restorative path. That's how it felt. That was the energy that came from her and her apartment. Healing. Restorative. Maybe purgative, but it is the season. And today is the day, right. So much to do, but this is so sad. Blessings, Detectives, blessings on you both," Delta Marsh replied.

"And she lived alone?" I asked.

"Well, yes, dears. Her and her goddess, but I don't mean that in an avatar way, like there was another person. Just that her home was also a shrine. It's not so strange, but as I said, she was very devout. Really going through something. Very positive though. Good healing energy."

We thanked the woman, and now knowing that there is no one to disturb in 418 with our entry we opened the door and went in.

The walls were at a permanent touch-up setting that enhanced the original aesthetic of the building and the room itself. The walls looked like sliced wood, like the walls were from a Pre-Katastrophe shack, inside wood clean and smooth. It felt warm and homey, and wafts of sandalwood and other incenses hung low in the air.

It was a big corner room with windows, but thick maroon curtains kept out the morning light. Electric candles flickered around an altar before a statue, 3-D printed from carbon, and painted to look like aged wood. The altar and shrine were the main focus of a room that otherwise contained a daybed with tossled pillows and blankets, and an intimate kitchen with table and one chair.

Why would someone live such a lonely life? I had the neighbors on my floor and everyone at work and my family. But maybe she has a full life elsewhere, wherever she goes at night that she comes back home from every morning at just after dawn. Maybe her home was just a shrine, and this was part of a devotion or penance, as her neighbor believed.

I turned my attention to the shrine. Was this all connected? Was this a Sacred chain of acts of violence involving 'Aho'eitu disappearing, Pearl Iko being killed in an avatar-training session, and Assata Yemi being killed right out in public on the street and then being carried off somewhere along with Pearl Iko's body? Maybe he was bringing them to where he brought 'Aho'eitu?

The altar seemed to be half on a windowsill and half on an antique wooden table abutting the wall and window. The shrine portion of the table spread out wide and allowed a place for Assata to sit and to utilize the table as a desk for writing and drawing. The maroon velveteen curtain kept the wooden statue centerpiece of the altar from the window itself—most likely a touch window and part of the building updates.

The statue was the center of the altar with five candles

equidistant around its base. The scent I got off of them was orange and cinnamon and some honey. Antique, reprinted peacock feathers crossed behind the statue. It was dark wood, accurately ancient looking, with spindly, squatting legs, but a large round belly and wide breasts resting on top, and a face with wide cheek bones, a high forehead, and a tight ball of curly hair that gave an expression of ecstasy, or was it care, or awe.

I looked down into the center of the shrine and I saw her. It was me. Dirty, brown hair pulled back into an exercise bun, but not too tight; pecan skin, with freckle-dusting across the nose bridge, cheeks, and forehead; a tightness at the brow and the corners of the eyes; upper lip tight against my teeth; and my eyes were so dark they held my gaze and made me want to cry.

For a moment there I felt like I had found something I was missing, but what I could not say. It was a good feeling.

On the rest of the shrine was an incense stand of clay in the shape of a sunflower. The incense stood in the center of the flower and as it burned the stem filled with ash. A mortar, a pestle. There was a strip of yellow linen and gold-colored bracelets. The mirror was the center of the shrine. The statue the center of the altar. I stood back staring at myself in the mirror until I took one more step and the ecstatic face of the statue came back to me from the mirror instead of my own.

I was most attracted to her writings and drawings. I was learning about the subject—Assata Yemi, a human, a citizen, gone to early and violently—by the design and decorative choices of her apartment, by her choice of goddess and practice of worship, but on the deepest, most personal level, from the works of her own hand. The drawings were simple and perfect, rivers and meadows, and her writings were mostly descriptive of the drawings.

On the corner of a wide piece of parchment paper, she had written out:

> *Sing of the wings, of a three toed frog*
> *Eat weeds from the deepest part of the sea*
> *Bring the trumpets from heaven*
> *And the fire from hell*
> *Then nobody can break the spell*

In the opposite corner she had written—in beautiful cursive hand—*Oshun*.

"That's…" began my partner from behind me.

"Oshun," I read out loud with no real intention.

"…Oshun," he said in harmony; and continued.

"She is an Orisha in the Yoruba pantheon. She is the goddess of love, forgiveness, motherhood, rivers, and streams. She rules over all that flows through human

107

connection and life in the world. It seems that maybe Assata Yemi was doing some healing here. This is a very reverent shrine, Edwina—" he said, kindly, almost awkwardly before finishing—"Casaubon.

"But look what I found in a box under the bed. I thought there was something familiar about her. It was a dreadful feeling, more dreadful in actualization. But look," he instructed.

Within the wide wooden box between his hands, an assortment of ephemera, but sitting on top was a printed photograph. It was immediately familiar. I had been in that scene, and I had seen those people. Dressed just like that, skinsuits touched up all black. Heads shaved short and then dyed black.

"The Abyssoids, or was it Voidoids?!"

"Names don't matter to them, remember. That's what they said. But maybe there isn't a *them* anymore?" speculated my partner.

"Assata Yemi is Crenshaw Maccabee," I said, as I saw it now, from what I could bare to take in of her face earlier.

"Assata Yemi *was* Crenshaw Maccabee, Casaubon. Please, allow her to move on. To grow, to transition," he reminded me. "It is said that Oshun feeds the hungry, Casaubon. It seems that after the period of nihilism, Crenshaw Maccabee was hungry for reciprocal love from her deity, or at least a belief system that allows it.

We looked up her name in the Archives and Census and confirmed that she recently changed her name from Crenshaw Maccabee. That was in March.

We looked up the other nihilists—the believers in Nothing—of the group, the Abyssoids/Voidoids, and found the address its phone number for Lucite Berenger, and then the same address and phone number for both Violet Burt and Tungsten Kung. We tried Lucite Berenger's number to no avail. Violet Burt answered at the following shared number.

We told her about Assata Yemi, and there was a sincere gasp and subsequent crying. We asked if we could speak to her and Tungsten Kung more in person and she invited us to their home in Douglasville.

Don't Deceive with Belief, Knowledge Comes with Death's Release

On the tram we surged west-southwest, and now at midday the spectacle that was *The Great Day of Mourning* was unfolding. It was beneath us, above us, and all around.

The buildings and tram towers were touched up in clashing, dissonant, multifarious ways, but all around themes of what we've lost re-presented through video footage from the Archive. Meadows, streams, forests, steppe, pampas, thriving deserts, the oceans, the seas, surfers riding on waves. Monuments by humans, and monuments to humanity were scattered more rarely throughout the clips and montages around us. Mostly it was the natural world, terms and situations I knew abstractedly in concept: tide pools brimming with active life, a mass exodus of bats from a cave, the Amazon River basin, boats sailing down the Yangtse River, climbers at a base camp of Annapurna, the cave towns of Australia.

The Citizens on the trams with us appeared to be heading home to these western suburbs before preparing and returning to the celebrations concentrated in the City proper. They were not dressed or touched-up like everyone I saw below. Below people reveled. Extravagant and ingenious costumes developed to mimic lost Nature. Clothing in honor and approximation of past cultures and traditions from around the world.

And I knew the chemical tools of illumination, both Profane and Sacred, were flowing freely. Medical aid was ready at all corners and inflection points of human movement on the streets and greenways. Mostly people would need hydration. Pulque and other libations, psilocybin in various tasty forms, cannabis in oils, tinctures, and delicacies savory and sweet. They would be flowing already at this time of day, and their ubiquity and potency would grow over time into evening. In the dark we will lose ourselves, and by morning we will have found ourselves again. It was *The Great Day of*

III

Mourning, and in our most healthy social response to this most tragic of all memories, we celebrate. We celebrate our triumph, our tenacity, our will to live, and our will to humbly heal ourselves, and rise out of and through this guilt, to somberly dream out loud and together about a better world, and then to make it, and live it.

"It is all like one big EDF," I said, looking down at a parade in the greenway of 285, stamping like an inch worm on the path through the crops, everyone parading touched-up to look like a segment of the worm. Directly below them on the streets people danced in free form chaos, spinning independent movements with no choreography or established rhythm.

"That is the idea on the most social and Profane level, Casaubon," said my partner. "This celebration is necessary for the greater good. The morale of a citizenry is as crucial as their appetites fulfilled, and often one results from the other."

"We should all lose ourselves to how glad we are in losing ourselves that we can return to sanity and prove we aren't really lost?" I asked.

He laughed, not so much at me, but at what I said or the way I said it, I hoped.

"It is your sensitivity, along with your rationality, that well-equips you for this work, Casaubon. As Plato reminds us in his dialogue, *The Phaedrus, the greatest blessings come to us through madness, when it is sent as a gift of the gods*. We have done this forever. The Rig-Veda describes the effects of the Soma plant. The earliest of religious practices show shamanic disorientation of the senses with the goal of illumination. Or it might be better to say, with the simple human goal of understanding something."

We both put our heads to the glass and looked down together. Our world is always beautiful, but it is undeniably a bittersweet beauty. The bitterness informing the sweetness was most pronounced today, in the motley, swirling chaos of life being lived on the streets and in the towers of our world. A day in remembrance of the discovery of our most fatal poison. We dance, sing, cry, parade, revel. It is our greatest Profane party.

"Now, we understand the psychological and sociological benefits of these experiences. What we are doing, and I am sure you have felt it every year on this day wherever you were, is palpable in a community such as ours. Sacred or Profane, it is all a form of sacrifice. The process is one of transition, liminality, purgation then shredding and rebirth. A Profane need so deep that we often express is as the Sacred.

"It is *carne-vale*, a time to say farewell to the flesh, to our mortal bodies, and remind ourselves who we are by throwing our identities into relief. We all need ego death at times. We are losing a part of ourselves that we don't need any more, that we have moved beyond, old ways of being, old versions of ourselves. It is all to learn something about ourselves. The only way we change and grow is through learning. Our bodies and levels of consciousness can learn even if we don't consciously realize it. We feel the change.

"The only worry is what Profane Prophet Walter Benjamin described as *the dialectic of intoxication*. Like with any substance, the dose makes the poison. And even with this, there can be too much. Especially with this. It is a dialectic that requires caution. The great risk of intoxication, or any explorations into the liminal is getting stuck. Your friends with the midday mind-away, 'Aho'eitu with the constant EDFs, the worry is wearing down the threshold. A desacralization of the liminal. And an overall desacralizing. Addiction is a form of getting lost in the liminal, and insanity and death await if one does not find balance within the dialectic," my partner concluded, and was interrupted, nevertheless.

"Believing in untrue narratives is also a form of poison on which we should not overdose, isn't that so, Rabbi Detective?"

Standing right behind us, in the aisle of the tram, was Noor Abbouchi, smilingly like a trickster. She was a friend of Thinkowitz whom I had met once before, also in transit. A worshipper of Sophia, the Neo-Platonist, gnostic embodiment of wisdom, and a general interrogator of belief whom Thinkowitz enjoyed sparing with. She worshiped Sophia, but made very clear that she does not "believe in her" in any material way.

"Hah!" Thinkowitz barked with surprise and joviality at hearing her voice and turning to see her there. She was wearing a fluffy indigo robe covered in constellations, and her umber hair was up in a wide loose bun.

"The literal truth of a belief system matters less than the practical or functional truth, isn't it Noor?" he replied.

"Psychological truth-value does not change the veracity of a narrative, especially one that is meant to be descriptive and believed in because of the applicability of the description of our world and the understanding that it brings," Noor Abbouchi parried and countered.

"Dealing with the specifics of today, regardless of the narrative dress-up, rebirth is one of our greatest psychological tools. And therefore, often considered a Sacred, religious act. It's a narrative understanding of a psychological need to grapple with an understanding of our mortality," went Thinkowitz.

"As conscious animals, what we are conscious of is our death. That is what sets us apart from other animals. And everything else follows after that, all worries, all religions, all delusions, all conflict, all evil," she said.

"So, the religious impulse is a psychological side-effect

of consciousness?" he asked sincerely.

"Spirituality came first, and it began with intoxication. Just a basic psychological response to disorientation. Deep inside a person shouts, *something is weird, aaaahhhhh, mystery exists, what's with that*? And then they start to ponder. Really just making shit up. And then next the religious comes from the two primal fears. Or were the two primal fears before intoxication and spirituality? Hmmm. Which came first?" she asked, quirkily, playfully, her clear blue eyes flashing their brightness as she smiled.

"Do tell," he chuckled.

"As humans our most primal fears are that we are afraid to be alone, and so we invent gods, and we are afraid to die so we invent a soul," Noor declared matter-of-factly.

"My god is real. I didn't invent it, nor did my ancient ancestors. I feel it, I know it in my bones, and I follow through by making the leap of faith. I wrestle with faith, because it is a wiggly and protean thing, but it is mine and it is real. And I believe Hashem gave you—us—the intellect to develop that theory about primal fears. It is a very good one," he said and smiled, truly enjoying debate. "My god works in mysterious ways."

"Or things just happen, and you are trying to wrap it all up in a convenient narrative because things not making sense is as scary as dying and being alone?" she posited.

"Maybe that's it, huh? We are just filling in abstraction with concrete-sounding stuff because we are scared to admit we don't know?"

It felt like they were putting on a show for me, or a show regardless of me. Playing a game with no end and no set gameboard or schedule. Heading to Douglasville from Assata Yemi's apartment I felt like we finally had a lead in this case—these cases—and my anxious desire to hold on to that ephemeral feeling of certainty built a tension in myself as we got closer to our destination, and yet my partner still debated with his friend like what we were doing existed in its own separate space. I didn't have the ability, or mental acuity to compartmentalize like my partner did. I still listened while I felt this and tried to focus on the words of Thinkowitz. I had a lot to learn, and my own anxiety, fears, and internal pressures to control the uncontrollable were standing in my way of this learning. Maybe I was also envious of how entertained Thinkowitz was by this other person? Someone who challenged him instead of merely listening and accepting.

I remembered something Thinkowitz told me after our first case together, *It is not our job to prove or disprove a myth, Casaubon. We respect the belief, and we try to build certainties out of the mysteries around us.*

We had passed 285 a while ago, and the tram followed the path of I-20, moving out of the City proper towards the western edge of our Domed-world.

—

Noor Abbouchi exited at the Sweetwater Creek stop, and hugged Detective Rabbi Jakob Rabbinowitz before she left the tram. She was sweet in her goodbye to me and clasped both of my hands in hers. She was as beautiful, sorrowful, and complicated as our world, and the lingering glow from her crystalline azure eyes lit the tram car the short remainder of our ride.

A Small Plot of Land

There were small, flashing glimmers of creativity in the suburbs. We all need it. But the Somber-Hope out there has a dense sullenness at its heart. People seem to huddle in their homes a little more, and the household gods and family pantheons are like domestic blankets of comfort. Especially today, coming from the City proper on this holiday to neighborhoods out this far. The creativity was here, but the contrast was obvious.

As we walked up the sidewalk a short rise from the tram pylon, we leveled out on Bambara Avenue and the buildings were only sporadically touched-up in vibrant digital decoration, but between some of the towering apartments and vertical ways of life, were low houses, a more common feature of the suburbs. All the people we passed were going the opposite way, heading to the trams to the City, although some of these outer communities had their own local events for today.

On the way down the tram lift, as we left the lingering image of Noor Abbouchi behind, the way she made me feel reminded me a little of Dayang Masalanta. But she was an avatar and Noor was professedly the opposite of that type of devotee. Maybe it was more just intelligent women, active in their own searchings, that stimulated me, not specifically the avatar aspect. And with Dayang it was definitely in part how she looked at me, her eyes, *and* the ways her hips moved.

Up on the right, we found the house, 457 Bambara Ave, and it was snug in-between two total height building towers. It was an antique original build of the Pre-Katastrophe, maybe as early as the mid-20th century, but remodeled to attract more light in its current arrangement. The three other houses looked similar and fit between each of the four building towers on this block. A shared green space sat between the four houses on the ground, and I imagined the towers had their own green levels for inhabitants.

It was a white house, narrow, two-stories tall and a vaulted roof of glass to capture light from an angle between the buildings and direct it into the house. Papier-mâché masks of monsters and monstrous gods hung from twine in streamers around the front of the house. They were each colorful and lively through their painted monstrousness.

Thinkowitz knocked, and immediately we heard shuffling and a soft, kind voice called out for us to enter.

They met us in the foyer and ushered us into the house, following to a center table. We could see straight through the house out the back glass wall into the green space, a playground in the center and garden boxes around the corners, and light came in from the large windowpanes of the front wall.

"Sit, sit, sit," she said. "I'm Violet, Violet Burt. Yes, we met before. Sit. I was just straining some strawberry juice and was going to make some tea. Juice? Tea? Detectives?"

We accepted beverages, juice for me and tea for my partner, as we sat at the table. Tungsten Kung introduced himself and shook our hands.

"We are happy to see you both—again," he added the last word almost a little sheepishly. "And you're very welcome here, but I, we, understand this is not a joyous visit. Or it is a nice visit for a not nice reason, maybe. Here, please, try some granola that we made earlier."

He put the earthen bowl before us, and his smile was sincere, but it also poorly hid his worry. She sat next to him on the other side of the table from us with steaming mugs for my partner and herself, and two glasses of radiant pink, sticky juice for Tungsten and myself.

Now I had the chance to really observe them. They were both larger than I remembered them. And lighter and brighter. It wasn't just the lack of all black clothing, it was them. She was clearly pregnant, and expecting soon —full and glowing everywhere—,and he had a big belly, thick thighs, arms, and a cute second chin rounding out his face. They looked wonderful, happy, and healthy.

There was music playing softly in the house, strings and birds singing—a classic my father played a lot when I was young—and looking around this was an abode of quaint activity. The supplies for the papier-mâché masks outside—the paint, paper strips, brushes, and glue bucket —were on the living room floor. A loom was in the corner with yarn baskets surrounding. A violin was on a stand in another corner. The ceilings were very high above use, exposing the elaborate system of glass panes that directed light throughout the house. The walls were white and looked painted. All of the furnishing was light-wood-colored pressed carbon and glass. In the living room, above a big soft futon was an art print by the late-21st century art collective MAAWAAM, a famous and common image of a drop of water zoomed in and pixelated beyond any representation, but still undeniably what it is.

"Thank you for this tea. And I am deeply sorry to be here to tell you about the death of your friend, Assata

Yemi," began my partner, but let his words hang in the light of the room for a moment. The couple before us breathed together in and out and then clasped hands.

Violet Burt put her free hand on her belly and spoke.

"It is a lot to take in. In some way, she was already dead to us, and at the same time we've been enjoying getting to know our new friend, having calls and learning about her. We mourned Crenshaw, and we trusted and respected her decision, so our friend was gone. That identity was no more. That's how she said it. A dead name. She was Assata Yemi now. Assata was her mother's name." She rubbed her belly and smiled and cried a little.

"Was it her leaving that identity that led to your group, the Abyssoids, breaking up?" I asked.

"No, it was mutual, for all of us, pretty much. I think it had run its course, what we needed from it. We felt like tricksters at first. Very punk. But it didn't take long to feel like brats, like we were troubling people for no reason. We both now worship deities who balance the trickster impulse, gods of the home, and domestic life. Safety. Comfort. He worships Kōjin, Japanese goddess of the hearth, and I worship Zao Shen, Chinese goddess of the hearth," said Violet.

Tungsten cut in, "We had all started to get a little grumpy. We thought we were having fun, but being confrontational with everyone in our lives or on the street was taxing and we didn't know it. At first. Assata was the first to voice concern, to notice how we all were getting. And right around then Violet realized she was pregnant. That instantly changed everything for both of us."

"This was late January, not long after we met you both," added Violet.

"When are you due," I asked.

"Very soon, this week, a few days after the new moon. June the first. Friday, so soon" She beamed and wrapped her arms around her very full belly. Tungsten leant a hand to the embrace.

"How did the four of you come together in such a way?" asked Detective Rabbinowitz.

"We met at a cafe in Buckhead with a reading group, a place called Oxford Books. The cafe had a Profane assortment of classical texts. I had gotten into the book *Dr. No* by Profane Prophet Percival Everett, and while the antiquated social tensions were almost incomprehensible, the indescribable concept of nothing at the center was really fun for me. As I read out passages to the others in the cafe reading room some laughed, and some walked away. Eventually, it was just us four. Those who laughed.

"And for Violet and me, it was also love at first sight." He leaned over and she met him for a kiss. Then he laughed, "but of course our love was nothing…"

"…but nothing beats something," Violet finished.

"And now we have something," he patted at her belly as a new beginning.

"So, Assata left first, and then shed her identity, took a new name, and started worshipping Oshun. What else has she been doing? Has she engaged in any community or social efforts?" asked my partner.

"Well, since March, since the new name, the rebirth, she committed herself to healing and redemption. On April 1st she committed to sincerity and began working efforts at Tartarus as a penance for how we bothered N'Deye Frimbo in the past. Why did he get to possess the void, Tartarus, we used to brattily complain. Assata was atoning for Crenshaw—Rest in Peace—and she was atoning for us too. She didn't worship Tartarus, but she cared for the temple. She worked night shifts there tidying, cleaning," said Violet.

"What can you tell us about Lucite Berenger? We tried his home phone, but he didn't answer, and there is no listed touch-tablet. What has he been doing since the group disbanded?" I asked.

"Yeah, the poor guy, he's had a life. And nothing really

meant something to him. And not in some semantic twist pun way. He really felt bold and proud believing in nothing. And I think that is because there wasn't much in his life that did mean anything, so he really embraced nothing. *Dr. No* hit him pretty hard. He was excited. His zeal that first day we met was what most likely drove everyone else in Oxford Books off," said Tungsten.

"He is so strong, really strong, and bolder than anyone I've ever met. He has a good heart, a loyal heart. He liked the confrontation, because he really believed in nothing as a thing. He liked it all. And he cared so much for us and the group that he respected the decision. Assata's mind was made up, and once I felt the pregnancy there was no turning back for Tungsten and me. Lucite respected it; he agreed. He said he did. He tried to put on a strong face. But we could tell he was hurt. That he felt betrayed, but we could tell he couldn't really face the idea that it was us betraying him. It was a little sad. We haven't seen or heard from him in a few months," said Violet.

"What is his background? Other than nothing what else held you four together?" I asked.

"Well, Assata had lost her mother not long before we all met last year. They weren't very close, and it seemed to cut her deeply, but not in any way she was ready to face. Both Tungsten and I lost our parents when we were young. And Lucite, an orphan since birth. We all grew up in different parts of the City, but working on the

Dome in some way or another. Both Lucite and I had worked in smart-glass production when we were teens, in different parts of the City, but we didn't know each other then. But it was fun to talk about those days and that work when we met last year.

"He worked in much rougher stuff than I did. Quarries and quartzite, demolition. He reduced hard rock to almost nothing. We liked the word *smithereens* together. It was really rough work though, but he didn't seem to mind. He was hard to reach sometimes. His childhood was hard, and he was most likely affected by some degree of damage from Dome-leak. And like most others he didn't have the advantage of a cyborg program."

She smiled humbly at my partner, awkwardly even, but with no note of insinuation.

I felt a little nauseated, but she wasn't wrong. And there should be a pylon at the top of New Gibraltar.

Sacred Detective Rabbinowitz began the subtle movements like he was going to stand, so we all followed. I took one last sip of my strawberry juice, and looked out the window wall to my right, a small group of five children ran through the green space, around the gardens, and with a pair of adults behind them, headed between this house and the adjacent building most likely towards the tram into the City.

Standing, we shook hands, and they both embraced both

of our hands in both of theirs in turn.

"When you speak to Lucite, please let him know that we miss him. That we hope he doesn't feel too betrayed or abandoned. Tell him that we love him. I think he really needs to hear that," said Violet Burt, and she and Tungsten Kung walked with us to the door.

The love I felt in their home was the literal opposite of nothingness. I was happy for them and felt true hope.

As we walked out onto Bambara Avenue, I was reflexively smiling and looked to my partner, and the shared feeling I supposed would greet me. However, he shuffled down the sidewalk ahead of me, hands in pocket, head down and hat low.

He called out, his words coming back towards me, over and around him, no other change in his fast, shuffling manner.

"Casaubon, what was Lucite Berenger's address, again?"

I took out my touch-tablet and unfolded it to a page-size and touched up the map.

"Lucite Berenger's apartment is located on Whitehall at number 340."

"What is the nearest cross street?"

"It is right at Whitehall and Windsor."

"Casaubon, fold-out your touch-tablet beyond just a page and expand the map. Keep a spot on Lucite Berenger's address in South Downtown, and touch a spot for Assata Yemi's apartment on 7th Street and Tartarus on 15th Street in Midtown

I did what he asked. Walking behind him towards the tram. His words kept flying back to me, but he never turned.

"Now touch a spot on the address of Mystical Embrace in the West End. How many blocks is it from Whitehall?

"It is three and a half, four really."

"And a block above Windsor, what street does Whitehall become, change its name to?"

"It becomes Peachtree Street." It ran as a roadway within those two names by or through all of these locations.

"Casaubon. I think I understand *what* happened, but I have as of yet, no idea *why*!"

And he was off and running, and I followed, trying to catch up.

The World Is Outside

We knocked vigorously and urgently on Lucite Berenger's door to no avail, and then went swiftly in.

The building was a relic of the 22nd century, an early design for supportive towers that are also living spaces. This building, along with those around it—jutting up through a tangle of overpass highways used as green space—once held up an early Dome prototype. Few people live in these buildings, and their function is mostly in support of the Dome. The apartment registered for Lucite Berenger was on the third floor at the level of the overpasses, made darker and ever-shadowed by those structures.

Through the thinness of the door, we were teased with potential discomfort within, but nothing could prepare us for what awaited. The sickly, sour smell of butyric acid filled our eyes, pores, and nostrils stabbing its dense airy tendrils into my stomach, drawing forth more of the same, and I held tight, choking back the reflexive wretch. My partner appeared equally affected and we both quickly smothered our coughs and covered our mouths and noses as best we could. My eyes burned, and we both squinted through the hazy, stale air. We avoided the light switches and Thinkowitz set his flashlight to wide covering half the room with each turn of the wrist.

Vomit was everywhere. Most of the major surfaces had some residue, either clear, dried, spittle foam, or thick, chunked with food, yellows, oranges, streaks of blood. Floors, the kitchen counter, the arm rest of a very old and threadbare couch—the only restive furniture in the one room apartment. The rusty steel worktable was free of this substance, but the surrounding floor bore biological specimens from someone's stomach. And it was very fresh.

The smells that overtook us were more than just vomit. Beneath that high, rancid note of butyric acid were stale notes of human sweat and bacteria mixed and agitated, along with the undeniable olfactory foundation of fecal matter. There was also an incongruous smell that I recognized from the cat enclosure at the zoo, a distinctive urine smell.

A toilet stood in the far corner from the door, and whatever lavatory-type space once surrounded it, had been removed sloppily. If the toilet had ever been white porcelain that was a very distant memory. It was crusted and streaked with blacks and browns. If the toilet was still able to flush, Lucite Berenger had made the choice not to employ that function.

Blood was visible on the floor in front of the couch. It looked like the blood had pooled and sat for some time, and then something was dragged through it spreading it out and leading to the door with fibrous striations.

It was a similar, personal simplicity to that of Assata Yemi's apartment, but instead of her organized reverence and obvious project of healing and self-care, this space was haphazard, random, and chaotic. The only visual concentrations of intentionality were on and around the worktable, even in the refuse littered in the pools of stomach acid.

We moved around the small space almost shoulder-to-shoulder looking at everything, sharing acknowledgement of various details with subtle nods and pointing. At the worktable my partner gathered together a loose pile of hand-flyers and paper announcements, the kinds of things that would have originally led Lucite Berenger to the Oxford Books cafe and reading room, and the groups that met there. Most of the crisp or crumpled sheets were about today and various locations for shared rejoice on this holiday— several of the largest EDFs included—and otherwise announcements for groups and events in neighborhoods adjacent to this building, including an assortment of avatar-training locations.

Thinkowitz lifted gently from its corner a hand-flyer for Mystical Embrace that read: *Come, connect with, and embrace what is ultimate for you. Become one with your worship. Nothing is a greater devotion.*

Otherwise, there was nothing personal, nothing that showed Lucite Berenger in relation or context with others. No photographs, no writing, no books, nothing. Only what looked to me like disassembled machinery. Tools, wires, empty pipes of different short sizes, small circuit boards, scraps of fabric and canvas straps, bags of flour labeled wheat and rye, sealed and labeled jars, sawdust, strips of aluminum foil, a soldering iron, and an array of beakers and graduated cylinders. Scanning and cataloging these components turned my glance to the sacks next to the toilet. Thinkowitz walked the few steps and peeked within.

"Fertilizer," he said.

I nodded in acknowledgement, but without understanding.

"Check the scent of those upright cylinders, Casaubon," he directed.

They were the source of the association with the cat enclosure at the zoo, and I told him that.

—

"Ammonia," he said, and I still didn't know what that meant.

This was the saddest room I had ever been in, and it was hard to think of this as a home. That a person *lived* here. The prime feature of our world, the world we have made, was connection, shared humanity, shared responsibility. Other than the machinery parts, and the visible sense of intention towards something that they denoted, it felt like there was no one or nothing really here. Nothing.

"…But what does it all mean?" I suddenly said out loud, regretfully uncovering my mouth and nose to do so.

"It means, Edwina, that we need to find Lucite Berenger fast. We are all in more danger than you could ever imagine."

They Followed None Too Soon

We rushed out of his building and turned north on Whitehall, and as it became Peachtree Street we were engulfed in the surging, joyous chaos. The streets were wild with mirth in every direction, and elaborate costumes and touched-up outfits were ubiquitous. All the touched-up glass of the surroundings buildings and towers brought a spectrum of colors and the natural world to every direction my eyes could take in.

There was no way to know where he was going. Or what he was doing, as my partner had yet to speak any more to me since we left the apartment. I converted anxiety into the strength necessary for patience.

My partner darted off to a corner, out of the cross-currents of people processing in all directions into and out of the five point center of the City there by City Hall in which on other days, not holidays, our City Council and chosen City Sovereign address our communal needs. He drew forth his own touch-tablet, something he rarely ever carried and unfolded it wide. From another inner pocket of his long black coat, he drew the photograph of the Abyssoids from Assata Yemi's apartment. He pressed the photograph against the tablet screen and then Lucite Berenger's face was in the tablet looking back at us.

I watched as Detective Rabbinowitz entered the image into the Digital Public Forum and held short of posting the image to all connected touch surfaces. He sent it instead to every personal touch-tablet and posted it on the Digital Public Forum welcome page. He included text that read: *Lucite Berenger; a potential danger to all; please tag location for Sacred and Profane Safety; keep a distance, and please use caution before placing gentle hands upon him.*

He started walking east on Memorial Drive, and I followed. We stayed close to the fronts of buildings and storefronts as the motley crowds danced up and down the street.

"We should have the ability to track everyone's tablets and buzz-wristwatches that are connected to the Digital Public Forum, or even use the touch technology to face outward as people pass, and that way know where someone is whenever we need," I offered, shouting over the din of my fellow citizens enrapt with the tragic joyous weight of surviving.

"That is a power no society should have, Casaubon, but I know you mean it in the most innocent and pragmatic way right now. Remember last night, at the BDMS. We monitor breath rates because we coexist and share all resources in this Dome. Our ecosystem works upon a very delicate balance. Accordingly, we have a census, and every life is known, and we are all essentially and necessarily linked to each other. Our society is as open and transparent as our Dome.

"Think of Cicero, in his work on laws, *De Legibus*, that you learned in school. He states: *Salus populi suprema lex esto*. The health of the populace should be the supreme law. Respecting the agency of a population is also part of the Greater Good. In respecting the sanctity and dignity of all life, we must respect all necessary aspects of life. This includes privacy. Trust is part of love, maybe the greatest part."

He had a way of projecting a clear, hard, whisper across space and distraction with the kind delivery of a teacher. As I thought of what he said his open tablet buzzed with a location tag and then another. The first to come in was a person who recognized Lucite Berenger's face in Parkview two hours ago, and the second had seen him in Glenwood Park almost three hours ago.

Thinkowitz hurried east down Memorial Drive.

"The tags are in the direction we've been heading. Do you know where he is going?" I asked.

"Not exactly. But I believe that he has killed at least two people—there is still some mystery—and that he intends to kill many, many more. Today is a day of mass congregation. But some locations are denser than others. Think of the trajectory up Peachtree Street from this morning, where Assata Yemi was coming from, and the direction it seemed he was taking her to, back to, with Pearl Iko. Tartarus, Casaubon. A place to dispose of bodies, or guilt, shame. But also, a void to fill. Remember, he is a true believer."

"But that is not the direction of the sightings that have come in," I added, hurrying after him.

"There are two enclosed Ego Death Fests today that are described in hand-flyers as the largest, although the expected estimates vary. The Galleria in Panthersville is the closest to his apartment, and consistent with the location tags so far. It is east of here and then south…"

But after the first couple, now the calls came in fast. Avondale Estates, Pine Lake, Pine Lake, several in New Gibraltar, all in the last hour. We saw a clearer trajectory, a direction in the locations.

"It looks like he is heading for New Gibraltar."

"And, Casaubon, what is the other biggest EDF in the City?"

"The Temple of Ninshubur Gardens!"

"Do you believe in coincidences, Casaubon?"

"I might be starting to," I said.

"That's a good answer. There's an express tram stop right above us. Let's go!"

Up we took the lift, and immediately caught a northeast bound express tram that was about the depart. We entered the last car and were off as we walked the length of the tram towards the front of the first car.

We were in pursuit. I heard Nina Simone's "Sinner Man" in my head, the fierce intention of the piano and drums, and it drove me. The rock, that white wonder, New Gibraltar, sparkled like a pearl in the distance, out of sight, at the end of this line. But we were heading to it.

There at the base of this our mountain, would be revelers, dancing, imbibing, losing themselves, and trying for that time to lose their *self*. Ego death. Entering a liminal space. Oblivion. Then rebirth.

We've got to run to the rock...

Friday, I thought Thinkowitz was referencing Euripides' *Bakkhai*, but here it was. At the foot of that mountain, we will find all manner of revelry and release, snakes twined in women's hair and staves of fennel, shaken and shredded. Horned-heads and costumes to look like pelts and fawn skins, and pressed carbon touch-fabric capturing the shimmer of Maenads in the wild. Dancing to music contained within through SAES sensors stuck behind the ear, but all of one beat, a pulsing beat of nature fecund and becoming, over and over and over again, surging.

All inhibitions gone, all connection to all life, all feeling within your body, so within your body you transcend it, your spirit passing back and forth through the porous membrane that separates spirit from body, through body. That is how I imagined all that I read in that ancient play, just last month, played out here in our world, and also from what I've heard, and the little I've seen.

In that play, there is a line about Dionysus being a god of prophesy that reminded me of our avatars. Tiresias explains, *His worshippers, like mad men, are endowed with manic powers. For when the god enters the body of a man he fills him with the breath of prophecy.*

Prophecy is another aspect people draw out of EDFs in general, but especially today. In some ways our New Year begins tomorrow, and this year there is a New Moon Tuesday, the day after.

But what would a nihilist, a devotee to literally nothing, find at an avatar-training session? My mind was finally asking the right questions that Thinkowitz had been leading me to.

"There is a strange irony to someone wanting to kill people who are already engaged in trying to kill their own egos," came out of me, and my thought process.

We were almost at the front of the long tram.

"The Ego Death Fest is part of the same imperative behind the world we've made. It is about recentering the self. It helps remind us that there is a world without us. But with us, it is a shared world, made for all of us, where we are all necessary and essential together. We all need that on a social, profane level, once a year at least, in a profound way. It is something we commit to daily. We've spoken about this before, how you feel it differently in the suburbs versus the City, but equally intense.

"Remember, along with Cicero, you learned in school the words of Profane Prophet Mariame Kaba when she teaches us about hope: *The idea of hope being a discipline is in conjunction with making sure we were of the world and in the world. That hope is a grounded hope that is practiced every day.* We all do this in the Profane through all of our efforts, and Dome-care, and community every day. Our lives are each and all daily practices of Hope, although a Somber-Hope, the hope of

—
141

those who understand the work, and the past that we have worked from and out of. Kaba also taught us, *Everything worthwhile is done with other people*. Our bodies physically, epigenetically, will not let us forget that. It underpins our world.

"This jibes with my traditions too, and that is why we have taken such a lead role in this project of continuing humanity. Our story is one of perseverance. I believe in the history of my people; our history is part of our faith. It is, one might better say, the reason for our faith. This Domed-world is the New Jerusalem of my people, for this is where we are, and wherever we are, and surviving, is our New Jerusalem. There was a movement in the 19th century of some of my people, Jews in a Bund, who believed in *doi'kayt*, a Yiddish term which conveys a sense of *hereness*, of being present in every aspect of existence. It was not dissimilar to Buddhist mindfulness, but it was meant on a larger social scale.

"This is our Promised Land, and it is for everyone, for if it is not for everyone, then it is for no one. Hashem, my god, is magnanimous in love for all humanity. I believe your god is the same."

I nodded in agreement and as an act of volition. We were at the front of the tram. I could see New Gibraltar in the distance. A shining whiteness, like emptiness, like potency.

All on that day...

"You spoke to the irony of killing people in the process of killing their own egos. You must have been thinking about what avatar-training, a connection with someone's conception of their own god, would do to someone who worships nothing, literally a void, the void, the abyss," said Thinkowitz, reading my mind like Dayang Masalanta. Where was she in this?

Thinkowitz went on: "I'm not sure you are aware, but responding to our Post-Katastrophe approach to belief, the de-abstraction of Kapital, there have been new studies of belief. The sociological midrash—a religious midrash from a sociological point of view—is that the ancient gods made us to provide them with food. Sacrifice, human or other. Writing came with agriculture. So, the ancient gods came with agriculture. And so, we based them on us. We are superior to animals and plants, and we cultivate them for consumption. We witness animals feed off other animals and plants. Life feeding off life. We imagine hierarchy, and we create a tier above us. It provides reason, or excuse, for when we fail, for chaos, for randomness, for fortune.

"This is similar to what Noor Abbouchi was getting at earlier. It is just another hermeneutic, a narrative device for looking, but might be useful in understand Lucite Berenger and the horror he brings," he said, but my fears seemed impervious to narratives of interpretation.

Don't you see I need you rock...

Fighting in the Dance Hall

I cried power, power, power Lord...

Dusk had deepened into darkness as we ran to the western entrance of the Temple of Ninshubur Gardens and collected caution before opening the doors.

The silence hung heavy within.

As we approached, the crowd had just parted in a radius around the middle with a single figure standing at the center point. He wore what looked like a fleece cloak, held tight at the neck and framing his head with a low hood. The rolling planters were mostly outside, but some remained in key areas around the large, wide space. My guess was for atmosphere, and the feeling of more life among life. There were easily over two thousand people inside.

The hood was thrown back, and the cloak dropped, revealing it to be no more than an old, filthy blanket. I could smell the vomit and sweat upon it above all the human odors contain in this place as we stood just within the ring the crowd created, about fifty feet from our subject, next to a bountiful, wheeled planter bed.

At the center of the Temple of Ninshubur Gardens, surrounded by thousands of citizens, frozen in revelry, panting and gasping, stood their would-be killer, Lucite Berenger. His clothes were almost rags hanging from his frame, barely anything left, but all of our eyes were on his torso. Pipes, wires, pouches, and a red blinking light. The explosive fulfillment of the parts on his worktable.

Everyone was still and quiet. Sacred Detective Rabbinowitz took a step forward, and stopped when Lucite Berenger spoke:

"I took those two lives to feed to the Void! They were an offering! I tried Tartarus. But I was stopped," he yelled almost every phrasing coming out of his mouth. He sounded angry and sad at the same time, pleading and threatening.

"Did he say two lives?" I asked my partner in whisper; he gave one nod and stared ahead. Berenger started to cry.

"All my life I've been told we are a community, that we are all one. Now I understand that this is something we need to do together. Gods need to be fed! You all get to feed your weak, silly gods. But what about ME, what about MY GOD! The oldest and hungriest of gods, the void, the nothing, it spoke to me, and it was hungry! It's our home to return to. It told me! Everything comes from nothing..."

Lucite Berenger gripped the wires and something else around the red blinking light with both hands. I felt my partner tense up next to me.
"Come with me! Please! It's time to leave the Dome! We are ready! The VOID IS READY! It fed so well before the Dome! So well! A feast billions deep! But it has grown hungry while we hide in here! No more hiding! IT IS TIME TO HATCH!!!"

"Smithereens!" My partner shouted, and Berenger turned his face in Thinkowitz' direction, and I saw shock, confusion, and a softening that followed, a flash of humanity as his brow lowered for a flash, and then started to rise again.

I'm the one always training, reading, running, engaging with calisthenics. But then to see *him*. To see him in action. A man of thought is a man of action. His body moved as swiftly as his mind. He grabbed a squash directly to his right, and his fingers snapped the vine immediately while the same hand lifted and adjusted the grip on the gourd.

Its stem was like the neck of a swan. His throw hooked it in the air with a snap of his wrist and it crossed the space, a yellow and green spotted gourd-fowl in tumbling flight right at the wide, flat forehead of Lucite Berenger.

He crumpled at once.

I felt the breath release from thousands of lungs while Thinkowitz and I ran to the center of the room. Lucite Berenger lay on the floor unconscious. The red light on the bomb continued to blink.

"Check the back," my partner ordered, as he pulled at all of the inflection points for the harness on the front. The back was equally secure, welded whole.

"It's not coming off. And there is no timer, it could go any time. We need to move fast. I don't think we can save him," he said.

"What are we going to do? Where are we going to go?" I asked.

The crowd was moving in closer around us all. Everyone looked concerned, ready to help.

"I know a place," said Dayang Masalanta, emerging

from the ring of citizens, her same white shift shimmering and snapping with her urgent movements towards us.

I was in awe without a moment for appreciation.

"Get him up!" Thinkowitz shouted, and the inner ring moved on Lucite Berenger.

"Gentle. Gentle," went hard whispers from everyone helping, and up he went, flat and high above everyone's heads in a cradle of hands, dozens. Thinkowitz and I were at each of his shoulders.

Dayang Masalanta led the way, and the crowd parted. She flowed fast between the bodies towards the eastern entrance, and we followed.

This group was dancers, revelers, trippers, purgers, and ego-killers, but that day, of all days, we were all mourners, and we were all citizens, so they—we-as-one —carried his unconscious body out of the Temple of Ninshubur Gardens like they—we-as-one—carried word of his sights across the neighborhoods of this Domed-world to this place not thirty minutes ago.

"The Mountain is here to serve," she called to us as we left the building and followed her on a path up the rise of rock. We were a careful and anxious parade.

Look at Those Cave Men Go

In the dark, this path to, and up, the rock of New Gibraltar would be hopeless without Dayang Masalanta before us. Trees, slopes, cracks, crags, and slippery slides of rocks were dangers in the night.

But we moved as one, a dozens-dense column, hands held to each other, and the hands of those in the center raised with the infernal and unconscious body aloft. Those in the front held small flashlights on Dayang, and her shimmering glow swished a path like a wandering star.

Going up and out of the woods we were soon joined by other revelers and pre-Dawn-worshippers, Sacred and

Profane, both. Followers of mountain gods, goddesses, spirits, deified-ancestors, and demi-monsters. Concerned citizens on our most joyous day of mourning. The Moon, flawed, almost full, anew two nights hence, was low over the highest pylons.

Any moment could be our last, and it seemed that everyone was feeling that, especially today, and while cautious of footing, this procession became one of controlled glee, with a zing in every move and exchanges of eyes, all around with shared nods and salutations. A low hum began, and I could tell it was a Bowie song, but it took me a moment to realize it was "Oh, You Pretty Things." Like "Life on Mars?" or even Profane Prophet James Hendrix's "1983 (A Merman I Shall Be)" it is the perfect ironic, bitter-sweet anthem for a day like today as we relish surviving past the worst hopes the ancients had for us.

Dayang Masalanta led us out to a small shelf jutting from just around the south side of the Mountain. As this shelf wrapped around out of the arbor-line, low shrubs and tree debris filled the space before us.

"This is a dangerous strip of narrow crevasses, some deep and some shallow," she said, but in the flashing of the lights, I could see nothing, but low, rough flora.

She went forward and pointed out a mound of leaf-covered branches and directed those closest to her to draw back the foliage.

"There. That is the deepest," she said. And as the lights flashed on what was uncovered, it looked like a terrifying place to have an accident. These coverings must have been placed by her as protections for people on the mountain.

All as one mind, we angled the lofted, unconscious body, radiant with menace and a lone blinking red light, and sent it down into the crevasse. A collective sigh was released, and I heard a smattering of prayers to various gods across dozens of languages.

We waited. We held hands and we waited. We cried, and I heard more prayers, and I said my own *Amen*, and we waited. No sound of bottom, no sound, but then...

The ground shook all of our footing and we gripped onto each other. The explosion was a bright red fireball down so far below it began as a speck, but we all backed up as a towering plume of smoke soon shot out. The mountain rumbled and shook, and we all could feel a little Dome-quake within us, our bones, and nerves.

Everyone wearing touch-clothing set their fabric to a low ambient glow and this whole shelf of rock jutting out of the mountain was lit like an early dawn. Some quiet prayers could be heard continuing, I hugged each person next to me in turn.

As the general silence left in abeyance after the bomb

actualized had started to fade, a low moan, and whine, and cry could be heard from somewhere deep and muffled. The adjacent clump of shrubbery contrived from leafy branches looked broken when I focused upon it, but my partner was ahead of me.

"Edwina Casaubon, over there!" he shouted and ran, and I followed with others.

"That's the shallowest one," Dayang said. And somehow arrived before us, as if she was moved through the mountain itself, and we three started pulling back the broken branches. Extra hands joining to quicken our reveal.

Another moan came from the crevasse that emerged into sight, and Dayang Masalanta reached her long, dark arm into the dark and drew back with a hand in hers.

We reached in and pulled out a sweaty young man, covered in soil, loam, sand, and pebbles. There was glitter all over his skin, sparkling up from beneath the packed clay. He gasped and coughed and heaved and breathed as we laid him down on the rock next to the cracked hole.

"It's Momo. It's Momo," was shouted over my shoulder.

I hadn't noticed, but Anurak Phonsavanh was with us and must have been at the EDF. He rushed to his friend.

We cleared everyone back, as hands brought us water and towels. We wiped at his face, and he opened his eyes.

"Momo, you're okay, you're alive!" said Anurak, touching his friend's hand.

"I had the strangest dream. I dreamed of the underworld, of Pulotu. I don't want to be called 'Momo' anymore. I'm 'Aho'eitu, call me, 'Aho'eitu. I am the son of a sky god and a woman of the earth. I am a bridge of the divine, the Sacred and the Profane," he gravelly gasped with a strange focus.

"Please, drink. You've been unconscious in the earth of the mountain for the last three nights. You are dangerously close to dehydration. Please, drink," encouraged Thinkowitz, holding the boys head up.

"So, no more worshipping avatars of Filipino mountain goddesses, huh, buddy?" asked Anurak.

After drinking two bottles of water and spitting up a little, 'Aho'eitu said, "Ha, yes, I'm so sorry I bothered her so much. I hope she doesn't hate me. I should apologize… after I rest." And briefly he did sound like the young person of his age, but still with a focus that seemed out of the character in his description from his sister and Dayang Friday.

"She's just…" I went to point her out, but my partner

stilled my hand. He shook his head and whispered, "she's gone."

"Let's not worry about that right now," Thinkowitz told him. "You will hear the story of last night for many years to come, but trust now that you are safe and balance is maintained." He drew out his touch-tablet, unfolded enough to show me, and went to the BDMS update. Three deaths today recorded. The first two were earlier in the evening and noted with names and natural causes. The third was the most recent and still of open details. Sacred Detective Rabbinowitz typed in the name, *Lucite Berenger*, and tagged this location.

A Godawful Small Affair

Dear Future, this is my report, my second case for the Sacred division of City Safety.

We all walked down New Gibraltar together. Someone had a blanket and we wrapped 'Aho'eitu in it and carried him gently down as a group. We gave him more water and nutrient packs, and City Safety medics met us at the bottom of the Rock. He was taken to his parents' home to rest in the most comfortable, familiar, and medically healthy way. The dawn was coming, but a newish Moon still hovered on the horizon.

"You have done well, Assistant Sacred Detective Edwina Casaubon," said my partner at the bottom of the rock, outside Temple Ninshubur Gardens as 'Aho'eitu was carried away. "Maybe we don't need the designation 'Assistant' in your title anymore. We couldn't have done this without each other. You have showed understanding that I could not teach. Your sensitivities and strengths have helped save lives. It is a mitzvah having you as a partner."

He hugged me, a rare event, and I hugged back.

"Now, I must go assure my family what they already know, they were safe all along, and I will always return home. Goodbye, Casaubon. See your friends. Get some rest."

Alas, Dear Reader of the Future, as you can see, our world is still a work in progress. But we are trying. I dream of a better world where no one is sacrificed for the Greater Good. A world without sacrifice for the Profane. Where sacrifice is only an abstraction of religious expression. We can't save everyone, but we try, and we all try together. I'm sorry we couldn't save Pearl Iko, and Assata Yemi, and Lucite Berenger.

Maybe in your time there will be a pylon up there, or maybe it's possible you found the greatest good in another way? Possibility nurtures hope. And vice versa…

Acknowledgements

As always in writing a book, there are many people to thank.

Firstly, my appreciation for Nate Ragolia and Shaunn Grulkowski of Spaceboy Books knows no bounds. Thank you both for continuously supporting me and my work.

San Grant, who created the gorgeous image on the cover, as well as the last cover in this series, who I've known since college, is a true visionary on paper and on film. Thank you for evoking my art through yours, Sam!

And then there's the family and friends: Ariane and Clint (and John and Catherine); Jon and Emily Polk (and Ada and Agnes); Gail Polk; Travis and Susie Burch; Tanya and Andy Frazee (and Cecilie); William T. Vollmann; Brian and Anna Grace (and Greta); Mounawar Abbouchi; Mike Karczewski; Tiffany and Rose Chameides; Skylar Nagao; Matt and Shawn McKinney; Neil Graf and Amy O'Brien; Mike Petri and Tara Biamby (and Liam); Kristin Hood; Bill and Crystal Brandon (and Quentin and Greyson); Molly Williams; Nick and Erin Maulding; Mark Hewitt and Fiona Reardon; Faisal Khan; Kai Reidl; Melissa Leahy; Adrienne and Amy Gandolfi; Adam Shprintzen; Ian

Campbell; Elizabeth Weintraub; Rachel McDonald; Christopher Nelms; Kim Kirby and Benji Barton; Sharmeen and César Hernandez (and Silas and Mia); Bobbi Jo Clarke; Ryan Alexander; and Miles Liebtag. I'd be dead without y'all.

And literary kinfolk: Pam Jones, Jeff Jackson, Erika T. Wurth, Joanna C. Valente, Duncan Barlow, Darius James, James Reich, Reginald McKnight, Ed Pavlic, Jarett Kobek, and Chris Kelso. Y'all inspire me. TKTKT TKTTK Either add more or cut this section.

And thank you to Jessica, Fox, and Søren: my heart embodied thrice.

About the Author

Jordan A. Rothacker is a writer who lives in Athens, Georgia where he received a MA in Religion and a PhD in Comparative Literature from the University of Georgia. He also received a BA in Philosophy from Manhattanville College in Purchase, New York, the state in which he was born. His essays, reviews, interviews, poetry, and fiction have been featured in such publications as *The Exquisite Corpse*, *Guernica*, *Bomb Magazine*, *Entropy*, *Vol. 1 Brooklyn*, *Brooklyn Rail*, *Rain Taxi*, *Dead Flowers*, *Literary Hub*, and *The Believer*. Rothacker is the author of the novels: *The Pit, and No Other Stories* (Black Hill Press, 2015/Spaceboy Books, 2022); *And Wind Will Wash Away* (Deeds, 2016); *My Shadow Book by Maawaam* (Spaceboy Books, 2017); and *The Death of the Cyborg Oracle* (Spaceboy Books, 2020); and the short story collection, *Gristle: weird tales* (Stalking Horse Press, 2019). 2021 saw the French language publication of *The Death of the Cyborg Oracle* and *The Celestial Bandit: A Tribute to Isidore Ducasse, the Comte de Lautréamont, Upon the 175th Anniversary of His Birth* edited by Rothacker.

For publishing news visit jordanrothacker.com.

About the Publishing Team

Nate Ragolia is a lifelong lover of science fiction and its power to imagine worlds more hopeful and inclusive than the real one. His first book, *There You Feel Free*, was published by 1888's Black Hill Press in 2015. Spaceboy Books reissued it in 2021. He's also the author of *The Retroactivist* (2017). His most recent book, *One Person Can't Make a Difference* (2022), was featured on Tor.com's Can't Miss Indie Press Speculative Fiction list, and was translated into Italian for Ringworld Sci-Fi in 2023. He founded and edited *BONED*, a literary magazine, and also created two webcomics. Nate is also a husband and a dog dad.

Shaunn Grulkowski has been compared to Warren Ellis and Phillip K. Dick and was once described as what a baby conceived by Kurt Vonnegut and Margaret Atwood would turn out to be. He's at least the fifth best Slavic-Latino-American sci-fi writer in the Baltimore metro area. He's the author *Retcontinuum*, and the editor of *A Stalled Ox* and *The Goldfish* for 1888/Black Hill Press.

Printed in the USA
CPSIA information can be obtained
at www.ICGtesting.com
LVHW042051011024
792665LV00011B/314